White Lilies in Spring

By: Reinelle Vespera

Copyright Page

Dedicated to the ketchup chip bestie.

And the ketchup chip hater too, I guess.

You know who you are.

Content Warnings

- This book uses Canadian English
- Attempted murder of a child
- Possible panic/anxiety attack
- Verbal abuse(?)
- Mentions of cancer
- Talks of suicide
- Talks of war
- Guns
- Stalking
- Mentions of racism
- Trauma
- Blood
- Daggers
- Mentions of being buried alive
- Missing children
- Ghost
- Mentions of affairs
- Violence
- Slight Gore
- Grief
- Death
- Funerals
- Mentions of dismemberment

Prologue

She was beautiful as she was dancing in the rain.
Droplets drenching her uniform as she sang a song from her youth.
Surely giving her a cold but the girl didn't care, for at that moment she
was happy.

She was beautiful as she twirled in a field of flowers, flowers so
lovely they resembled her smile.
Her cheerful dancing, enchanting those around her, including her
partner.
A boy her age, dancing with her.

She was beautiful as she laughed.
It was a hearty laugh, her friends by her side.
All laughing and smiling without a care in the world.
The calm before the storm.

She was beautiful, even as she cried.
Even as tears fell from her eyes which showed nothing but malice.
Her mouth moving but no sound coming out.
Yet her anger, so raw and apparent it sent waves through everyone
around.

She was beautiful.
The most beautiful woman I've ever seen.
Why would such a beautiful woman be so sad?
So angry?

So filled with bloodlust?

I groan as my eyes sense the rising sun, the summer vacation coming to an end. "What a weird dream..."

Chapter 1

Today's The Day

I shift out of bed, slowly but surely. I rub my eyes as I hear a knock on my door, "Emilia, I let you sleep as long as I could. You have to get up, today's the day you get examined to see if you're eligible for Reverie Academy."

"Yes mom, I know. I thought you didn't want me to attend the Academy?" My mother sighs, she walks towards me and sits beside me on my bed. I clench my purple duvet, expecting to be let down. She hugs me.

"I don't, it's dangerous and I don't want to lose my only daughter on the battlefield... I already almost lost you twice. I just...I don't want anything bad to happen to you. Nightmares are terrifying creatures and being a Reverie is a big sacrifice." My gaze softens as I try to show my understanding. I hug my mother back.

"I want to be a strong Reverie just like Oppa, even though he's not technically one yet, he's still super strong!" My mother smiles at me and nods, she gets up from my bed and tells me to get dressed so we're not late. I look at my beige walls, covered with artwork. There's lots of colourful pieces gifted from family. I get out of bed and quickly get dressed in my "uniform." I choose to wear a navy blue dress. They call it a uniform but it's more like a dress code since we can wear whatever we want as long as it's navy blue or white.

I go downstairs and see my father smiling, he's drinking a cup of coffee. I smile back as I walk up to him and mimic his excitement for today. He ruffles my hair and says "You're gonna be eligible for sure kid." I nod with a smile to show happiness and excitement. I feel a weight on my head, it's my brother. He's very tall. His lime green eyes stare at me affectionately.

"Oppa! Are you going to the academy today?!" I exclaim enthusiastically.

"Yep, sure am kiddo. Sorry we couldn't talk more, between your camp and my staying at my moms we haven't had much time to catch up." he smiles warmly at me.
He continues, "Your hair got longer, just a year ago it was barely covering your head. Now it's at your ears. You got taller too, doesn't change the fact that you're still a little shrimp though." I scrunch my nose to show annoyance.

"I'll have you know I'm one hundred and thirty-eight centimeters now!" My brother laughs and pats my head, he grabs his water bottle on the counter, then his bag at the entrance. He pushes his glasses up and takes out his phone, turning on the camera to use as a mirror so he can fix his ebony hair.

"After next year I'll be a full fledged Reverie."

He smiles and I smile back before he resumes, "You'll be going to grade six next year. Hopefully you'll be able to join me at the Academy. Even if we're only at the same school for a year, it'll still be nice to see you more often." I nod eagerly to show excitement.

"By the way, did you dye your hair? It looks like there's a bit of a purple hue to it."

I stare at my brother, confused. "Nope, maybe the sun bleached my hair or something? Cate says that can happen sometimes." He nods and a question pops in my head.

"Have you ever defeated a Nightmare before?"

He laughs and says, "Of course I have, what do you take me for? I've even defeated a calibre nine Nightmare."

"WOAH, REALLY?! Calibre nine is like the highest rank!" I respond, in awe.

I guess my brother found my 'excitement' to be funny cause he laughs. "Calibre 10 is the highest. Don't worry, if you get into the Academy you'll be busting Nightmare as-" my dad clears his throat, a sign that my brother shouldn't swear.

Regardless he continues "Sorry. You'll be kicking Nightmare butts in no time. I have a strong resistance to potential Nightmare spawnings so you probably will too. I also have a good amount of magic so you probably will as well. Well, I at least expect that you'll have a high enough resistance count and mana points to be eligible for the Academy." My brother looks at his phone before patting my head once more.

"Now I really got to go, tell dad how everything goes and I'll send you a letter once I hear the news." He says his goodbyes to our dad and my mom before heading towards the meeting place where he and his classmates will be warped to Reverie Academy.

Chapter 2

A Brush With Death

Right after Oppa leaves we start getting ready to go to my school, St. Michael's X Aetherist School. I grab my purple backpack, hearing aids and my orange water bottle before rushing out the door so I can get in the car. The drive is only 20 minutes but it feels like forever. I think my mom noticed my apparent anxiety since she tries to reassure me that things will be fine but we're already late so it doesn't do much to soothe me.

Once we get there my mom walks me to the main office and wishes me luck. She hugs me tight and kisses my forehead before heading back to the car as I walk down the tiled floor of the hallway. I speed walk to the gymnasium where evaluations are taking place, passing the washrooms and the walls with all the graduate photos. Obviously not wanting a teacher to stop me since I'm already late. Once I'm past the office, I start running towards the gym, sprinting up the steps, wheezing a little as I get to the top. I pass some empty classes. It's the day before the official first day of school so only us new grade five students are here today. I arrive -out of breath and wheezing- one of Reverie Academy's scouting assistants comes up to me. We stand in front of the blue metal doors that lead into the gymnasium. She looks kind, "Hello dear, are you here for an evaluation?"

"Yes, of course! My name is Emilia Jang, I'm so sorry for being late!" I give a slight bow to show respect, a reflex from going to my grandparents house...arghh this is awkward. I should really go out more...

The assistant smiles and extends her hand. "It's nice to meet you, Emilia." I shake her hand and her eyes immediately widen as she reaches for the dagger on her side. She's gripping my hand, hard.

"What are you doing? Hey, stop! That hurts!" She only grips my hand harder, as if she's trying to crush my bones.

At this moment something is telling me that here, right outside the gymnasium, if I don't do something I'll die for sure. Although, it's not like anything will change even if I do die. Maybe this is fate or perhaps destiny? I survived death before, I survived twice. So why now? Why is this happening to me? Although if I die here it'll be an inconvenience to others around me. I guess it's decided, I'll claw my way to survival if I have to. Just like before. Should I use magic? Wait no, I can't just use my magic inside the school. But also, what's the point in Specialty Magic if you don't show it off? Wait, what if I have Void Magic? I thought I was just being paranoid. There's no way I have Void Magic, I'm not a Nightmare! There's no way I'm a monster! Although my magic has been getting dimmer. I mean if you compare my magic to two years ago it looks rather pathetic in comparison. It's not like I have Inherited Magic do I? I've gotten surgery before but I don't think I've had a core transplant. Well...I've definitely had transplants before, two if I'm keeping count but a magic core transplant wasn't one of them! Oh wait, I'm literally about to die aren't I? Just before her hand could reach the dagger, my survival skills kick in. The dim light pooling at my feet solidifies, dashing for her neck in order to enact a stalemate. I hear footsteps coming our way, am I being saved or am I gonna get killed for real?

An elderly voice speaks up in a calm manner. "What's all this commotion?" Oh no, this is bad. Or good? I'm not sure but the guy I assume is the Elder that came to do our evaluations just walked in on me 'trying to kill' his assistant!

"Sir! This young girl here is a Nightmare! She has traces of Void Magic! She must be exterminated at once!" She lets go of my hand and pleads with the elder, I bring my wrist to my chest and rub it. A bruise beginning to form.

The expression on my face must be quite silly looking since the elderly man chuckles and only looks at me with kindness as he says "Nightmare? All I see is a cornered animal, baring its fangs in defense." My eyes widen in surprise, is this guy making fun of me or is he on my side?

He gets to my level "Hello, little one. I'm the Elder who came to evaluate the new grade 5 students today, would you like to be evaluated?"

Chapter 3

I nod and thank the kind Elder who came to my rescue, he introduces himself while smiling. "It is no problem, young child, my name is Atticus. You remind me an awful lot of a girl who used to go to the Academy back when I was the principal there..."

Ok, weird. What's that girl have to do with me? He didn't even teach that girl. But... he looks kinda sad, I shouldn't press further. It must be a hard topic for him.

He leads me into the gymnasium where my classmates and friends are. The white tiled floor and the blue brick design on the walls give me a feeling of nostalgia. The only thing different is the light coloured streamers and balloons scattered across the walls of the gymnasium. Thankfully it's just our grade here since only two hundred people are allowed in the gym at a time according to the fire department paper thing on the wall but our principal likes to shove all six-hundred plus students in here during assemblies. I obnoxiously wave to my friend Anwen as I follow Atticus up the white tiled stairs to the stage, much to the displeasure of his assistant who narrows her eyes at me. He continues to lead me, bringing me onto the stage. A mysterious object is placed in the middle.

This is the object that's supposed to read my resistance and mana level. This is it, this is the moment I've been waiting for, for years! I look up and immediately deadpan as I realize that, instead of some magical orb or mystical object it's literally just a printer. Atticus notices my clear displeasure and laughs.

"Just place your hand on the 'printer' and let it examine your magic and Nightmare resistance. Your results will be printed onto a piece of paper. As you know, resistance is measured from zero to five and mana points are measured on a scale of zero to one-hundred." I walk up to the printer and place my hand on it. Feeling a little cocky, I decide to make a show out of this. Grinning at Atticus's assistant knowing that this would annoy her further. Dimly lit light surrounds me, the printer beginning to do its work. Finally a piece of paper emerges from the printer, Atticus looks it over and his eyes widen. His assistant, wanting to see what's the cause for such shock, looks at the paper. She too is bewildered and honestly a little scared.

Huh? What's happening? Why aren't they showing me my results yet? I look on towards my friends, the kids, and staff in the gymnasium as they all must be wondering why my paper hasn't been handed back to me. I sure as heck am.

As I look around the crowd of sixty kids and a couple teachers, I make eye contact with a weird boy with rosy coloured eyes that I've never seen before. He must be new. While everyone else seems to be in a state of confusion, this guy is looking right at me, scowling. He's pretty, I guess. To others he may have stood out for his rich ochre skin and his pretty appearance, not to mention the way he carried himself. All I can see is that awful scowl on his face. Atticus hands me my paper. I guess I'll finally see why everyone is so flabbergasted. I see it the second I start reading. Written on the paper is a 4.95/5 resistance level and the number 1000/100 indicating mana points.

Atticus clears his throat and everyone's attention is back on him. "I am pleased to tell you that you have no reason to fear, dear child."

The crowd starts murmuring in confusion as Atticus whispers to me "You are the Saviour, little one. Take pride in your new role, for you will fix the world. However be cautious of who you reveal this information to, we cannot protect you if you're not attending the academy." I look around and smile at this new revelation. I nod. I wonder what he meant by not being able to protect me.

I look around and see the assistant who literally tried to kill me. Her face filled with the horror that she almost killed the Saviour. I mean I know being the Saviour is a big deal but I guess it's a bigger deal than the history books make it out to be. My eyes continue to dart around the room, I lock eyes with the boy who was scowling, only to see his face is contorted into a deep look of displeasure. I immediately look away. Ok ok ok, cool cool cool. This kid is definitely upset and I'm not afraid at all. I am definitely not afraid at all

I look at Atticus with wide eyes as he tells me, "You may not be very proficient at Aether Magic, but your mana points indicate you are undeniably the Saviour. In fact you are the second strongest in history." he smiles down at me.

I pause, obviously curious. "How strong was the strongest?" Atticus laughs.

"Already thinking of surpassing her, huh? Well she was the first Saviour and she had ten times your mana level so settle down little one." Atticus laughs again as my face immediately scrunches up in displeasure. He hurries me off the stage and beckons the next child to come up. Well that was simultaneously over and underwhelming. I guess I was whelmed? Mid-whelmed? I don't know. I look around and notice the Elder is looking at someone. Wait... is he making eye contact with the scowling boy? Did the Elder just freeze up? Do they know each other?

As I start wandering around the crowd, looking for my friends, I bump into someone, "I'm so sor-"

"Not only is the new showy Susie clearly lacking, but she's also unable to navigate her surroundings? What a joke." I tilt my head up, then down. Oh great, it's the scowling boy.

Chapter 4

This kid must be at least a third of a ruler shorter than me. Does he have no fear? I'm obviously a lot taller than him. Trying to get back at him I exclaim "At least I'm not vertically challenged!" The boy only looks at me with confusion on his face, his scowl disappearing as if he's trying to figure out what exactly I just said.

The boy then takes a deep breath and with a cocky look in his eyes he says, "I'm not quite sure what you're trying to prove by using roundabout language but if you're going to insult me at least do so using some level of intellect, although I'm sure that'll be quite the arduous task for an imbecile like you."

I, doing my VERY best not to alert the kids next to us, start muttering to myself, "Violence is not the answer, violence is not the answer, violence is not the answer."

"Hey Emilia! Congratulations on being eligible."

I turn my head and smile at the familiar voice, "Anwen! Hi!"

The boy, clearly displeased, scowls in response. "Didn't your parents ever teach you that it's ill mannered to interrupt a conversation so tactlessly? Or are you just as devoid in intellect as this sad excuse for a Reverie candidate?" My friends start making their way over to us and see what's going on.

Anwen smiles maliciously, "Didn't your parents ever tell you about common decency? I don't know where you're from but let me make this clear, being a jerk to people, especially to someone more talented than you, will get you nowhere. So, maybe think about that before you run your mouth about things you know nothing about."

The boy, clearly upset, starts to respond when he's suddenly interrupted by two girls, Diana and Catarina in our friend group, dragging Anwen away and trying to stop a potential bloodbath, not to mention avoid making a scene. The third girl, Alice, skips behind them with me. I guess the scowling boy was too stunned to speak because he just watched us leave.

As soon as we enter the hallway, Alice, Catarina and Diana, start exclaiming.

"Congratulations Emilia!" Catarina exclaims.

Diana follows, "Yeah, congratulations!"

Alice rolls her eyes, "What's that guys problem?!" I just laugh and thank them.

I look up in thought, "Yeah I wonder what that guy's problem is, I don't think I did anything to him. He just started making faces and insulted me." Diana and Catarina both assure me that I shouldn't worry about it and that he's probably just jealous

Alice laughs, "It would've been an exciting first day if you guys caused a scene! I could tell you and Anwen were trying not to punch that guy!"

Anwen sighs. "Causing a scene would be really bad. After all, that brat isn't someone you wanna mess with."

We all look up at her, confused, Anwen continues, "I heard from my parents that the Petrova Reverie family just got a new member. Turns out the head of the family, Matthew Petrova has a son named Damon. Although it's strange, my parents are friends with Mr. Petrova and he only mentioned he has a biological son yesterday who's mana control is apparently below average. There's only one other new kid in our grade, I think her name was Kala. That means Mr. Nice and polite must be Damon, not to mention he looks a lot like Mr. Petrova..." Right, the Lupo's are also a well known family, albeit a lot smaller... sorta. So that means they're definitely well connected

"Yeah he seems strange. I told him he's vertically challenged and he was confused by what I meant." I say.

Diana laughs. "To be fair, you say some pretty strange things sometimes." We all take a moment to ponder the existence of the scowling boy named Damon Petrova but eventually we decide it's not worth it.

Alice decides to break the silence first, "Wait. Guys, what score did you get? I got 61/100 mana points and level 3.8/5 resistance."

Anwen sighs again. "15 mana points and level 5 resistance. So at least I got that going for me..." We all look at her with sympathy. It must be rough being a member of the Lupo family and having only 15 mana points.

Diana decides to question me next. "What about you, Emilia? What'd you get?"

Uh oh. What do I say? I can't just say that I'm the Saviour! "Oh, we don't actually know." I laugh awkwardly, my friends look at me in confusion. "Something was up with the printer so I'm not really able to read my results. I'm eligible though so I'm happy about that."

Catarina responds. "75 and 4.2 for me."

Diana smiles. "That means we're all gonna be in the same class tomorrow as academy candidates since I got 58.5 and 3.5! Although, don't mention your scores to Silvia. She left early 'cause she got 44 and

2.6 she seemed really upset." We all nod in agreement. Not wanting to cause problems with Silvia.

~~~~~

The examination schedule finally comes to an end. I rush out the school, the concrete ground beneath my feet letting me feel more in control than if it were grass. I very nearly run into the chain link fence on the way to my mom who came to pick me up "MOM! YOU'LL NEVER GUESS WHAT HAPPENED!" I exclaim. My mom looks at me kindly and smiles while standing outside her black SUV. Hopefully she wants to hear how things went, the topic of Reverie's has always been difficult for mom.

"Wait!" A man runs up to us and lowers himself to my level. I look at the man, then to my mom. She looks really surprised.
"Hello, I apologize for startling you but are you Emilia Jang?" My mom immediately looks towards me with shock. I nod at the man, he looks familiar.
"My name is Matthew Petrova, I'm the father of the boy who picked a fight with you." Huh?! My eyes widen as I realize that Anwen was right, Damon really does look like Mr. Petrova... My mom is starting to look really nervous. Well, we are in the presence of one of the most famous Reverie's around. Mr. Petrova notices my mom's distress so I guess he decides to speed up his plans. He calls for Damon who begrudgingly walks towards his father.
~~~~~

"On behalf of the Petrova family WE.." Mr. Petrova grabs Damon's wrist "...are sincerely sorry for what transpired today. Now it's your turn Damon."

Damon rolls his eyes and says "I apologize that I insulted your intelligence before assessing the level of your stupidity."

Chapter 5

Today Is A Good Day

Oh...so that's how it's gonna be...I smile at Damon with as much displeasure as I can muster, as if to say 'This isn't over yet.' However I do thank him for his apology. He glares back at me in response. Mr. Petrova lets out an exasperated sigh as he apologizes again. He grabs Damon and leaves, making sure to scold him as they walk towards the other members of the Petrova family. I look up at my mom with a smile, only to see she looks...sad. She's smiling but it's not a happy smile. It's as if she's trying to hide her sadness. As we get into the car I buckle up and begin telling her what happened with Damon, how he glared at me and insulted me.

I was expecting her to scold me for insulting him back but she just says "That sounds like an eventful day..." It takes us fifteen minutes to get home. Fifteen minutes of pure silence, once we do I see my father. I hurriedly put my backpack down and take out my lunchbox before putting it on the counter.

I run up to him and before he can ask me about my day, I tell him in my most excited voice "THEY TOLD ME THAT I'M THE NEW SAVIOUR!!" My father smiles brightly, his face beaming with pride.

"That's great Emilia! You finally got your wish! This is pretty much a guaranteed entry into Reverie Academy!"

He turns to my mom who's still trying to mask her sadness, "Isn't this great?" I smile at my parents, the tension is palpable but I do my best to ignore it. My mom's face is paler than normal. I look back at my father and try smiling brighter, trying to fix the atmosphere.

"They said I have the second highest amount of mana points of all the Saviour's! Also, also, they said my resistance is 4.95/5!"

My father hugs me tightly. "You'll be the best Saviour, I just know it. You should go and change out of your uniform so you can wear it tomorrow."

I continue to smile despite my discomfort and say "It's not a uniform, it's a dress code." He chuckles and tells me to run along so I do. I go up the carpeted stairs to my bedroom. I go over to my dresser and change out of my 'uniform.' Despite being out of breath and wheezing from the climb up, I can handle being out of breath for now if it means more good days to come. I pick out a comfy shirt and some pants. The material hanging loosely on my unfortunately short stature. Once I've changed into my comfy clothes, I start to make my way to the stairs, the carpeted floor masking the sounds of my footsteps. As I'm about to take my first step down I hear it. The booming sound of a voice this house knows all too well.

"WHY CAN'T YOU BE HAPPY FOR HER?!" My father's screaming again.

My mom does her best to defend herself saying "I am! But I don't want to see my only daughter be nothing more than a weapon! She can barely run let alone fight!" My breathing quickens and my vision starts to get muddy, everything starts feeling far off. There's a lot of yelling, too much yelling. Why now? Why today? The last thing I hear is a bang, I guess my father started slamming things. Everything blurs together and eventually I end up in my closet, holding my legs up to my chest as tears stream down my face. The pressure building up is becoming too much. My head spins. It's all my fault...if only I was normal or even someone like Oppa...then my parents wouldn't be fighting... somehow I muster enough awareness to create a dimly lit dome around myself, it's not soundproof but it helps, makes me feel safer... I rock myself back and forth, a silly attempt at trying to soothe myself. A familiar figure in the corner, smiling down at me.

"Remember what you promised." It's strange... has my magic always been that dim? I thought it was brighter than this... well... It doesn't matter now. I'm not sure how much time passed before I finally look at the figure in the corner.

I look at her, or should I say IT in the eyes and ask "Why do you hate me?"

"Don't you remember? You still haven't paid me back for the price of your existence, number eleven."

Chapter 6

A new day arrives and I'm completely drained. The events from the night before left me tired and shaken, yet I still get ready for school. Putting on the same navy blue dress, the September heat of Toronto being too unbearable to even think of wearing pants. I go through the motions of my everyday routine in a daze. Not really registering my surroundings or what's going on. I arrive at school in a blink of an eye. It's 8:45 am, school starts at 9:00. I walk into the yard, play structure in sight. I head for the base of the blue slide.

"So, who's that asshole you were talking with yesterday?" I jolt back to my senses and turn to see my friend, Silvia.

I sigh "You shouldn't swear at others so loud." Although I've gotten used to Silvia's rather foul use of language -something she picked up from her older brother and sister.- I don't want to get in trouble 'cause she can't swear quietly.

She rolls her eyes and crosses her arms, I sigh "Anyways, his name is Damon Petrova, he's part of the Petrova Reverie family."

Silvia's eyes widen "That means he's rich. Like, REALLY rich."

"I mean I guess, but what does that have to do with anything? He's still a jerk." I try to reason with Silvia, knowing exactly what she is trying to get at.

She rolls her eyes, "Just watch as I reap the benefits of being his friend. I mean I deserve that much since my mom uses all her child support money on herself. Plus, I literally live in the hood." As much as I want to sympathize with Silvia, it's a little strange that Silvia's mom supposedly uses all the child support money on herself yet Silvia and her siblings were always more than well provided for. That much is obvious based on her shoes and how often she bought useless trinkets online. Not to mention I've been to Silvia's houses before, both her moms and dads, and both definitely have money. I guess the difference between what I see and hear makes me doubt her. As much as I don't want to believe Silvia is lying, it definitely felt odd how her 'selfish' mother who "exclusively spent money on herself and not her kids" simultaneously spoiled them rotten.

~~~~

9:00 am rolls around and we all start walking up the six flights of stairs. Kids start piling into their classroom. Me and Silvia meet up with Anwen, Diana, Alice and Catarina in our new classroom. Lucky for us, we're on the top floor, yay. We love climbing six flights of stairs. A woman just below what I assume is average height, stands at the
~~~~

front of the classroom, her black hair and glasses gave her a stern vibe consistent with the rumours surrounding her.

"Hello class, I'm Ms. Carvenon and I'm your teacher for this year. I'm aware that you all must be incredibly excited to be selected as our schools potential future Reveries in training. However I will warn you that the requirements needed to actually remain in this class for the whole year is not something just anyone can achieve. If I feel you are unfit to enter Reverie Academy next year, you won't even make it to the lucid ceremony. To be frank I will simply transfer you out of this class. Are there any questions?"

It's like I can hear all our eyes widen with shock. We heard that Ms. Carvenon was strict but I at least, didn't think she would actually transfer us out of her class mid year. I guess we all just assumed we'd make it to the Lucid Ceremony at the end of the year. Even if we don't get a Lucid Crystal, we've all been waiting for that ceremony. We all just wanna see what the school ID to the Academy looks like. She didn't even let us take our seats before dropping this huge bomb on us!

"Oh and I will warn you. As you know at our school, bullying is prohibited, however this rule is even more strict at Reverie Academy. The Academy will not accept any form of bullying and will kick you out without hesitation if they find you have been bullying others. My job is not only to teach you but to weed out anyone who thinks it is acceptable to torment others. The Academy places high values on honest and kind individuals, with that being said, you are allowed to report your classmates for things you deem as offensive. However if they are found to be false, you will be punished instead and depending on the severity you may be kicked from this class." The class stays silent and continues listening, hanging on every word.

"The morning subjects will usually consist of your usual academic material you would learn anyways, while the afternoon subjects will consist of new material you'll be learning in preparation for your hopeful entry into Reverie Academy. These subjects will include the basics of magic and poisons, as well as simulations to test your ability to think under pressure and pain tolerance, lastly I will also be giving out tests. We may have some special guests come in occasionally, so your classes with them will depend on their availability." Ms. Carvenon leaves the room, I'm guessing to grab her teaching materials from across the hall.

Silvia gets close to us and whispers with a smile. "So what I'm hearing is, we can eliminate each other from the candidate list?"

We each look at her with shock, save for Anwen who stays silent, as if recalling something then says "It's true, Anastasia told me one guy got eliminated for trying to sabotage her friend back when they were in their training year."

We all stiffen up, except for Silvia who says "I know exactly who I'm going to get kicked from the program."

Chapter 7

"Now, if you don't have any questions let's start the first lesson. While you normally learn this in your first year of the Academy, I decided it'd be best to learn some history seeing as it's important to know of the past so as to not repeat the same mistakes. This way you can all better analyze trends." My classmates all picked their seats as Ms. Carvenon starts writing on the board. Me and Anwen sit beside each other at the front of the class. We're in the corner where the blackboard and whiteboard meet, Catarina and Alice are in the row beside us and Silvia and Diana behind us.

As soon as we get settled the first class of the morning began, "What do we know about the Saviour?"

One of the guys raises his hand, he's a year older than the rest of us due to him missing the previous years examination, "A Saviour is a girl who has Aether Magic with an MP of over 100. Likely someone outside the Chevalier family." We all look at each other in agreement, wondering why Ms Carvenon isn't saying anything.

"You're on the right track, however that is the explanation given to the younger kids. Now that you're older it is expected that you know the true definition. While what you said about Aether Magic and MP is correct, however defining the Saviour as a 'girl' would be incorrect. A Saviour is defined as someone whose estrogen is higher than their testosterone. Your comment about the Chevalier family is correct however. Statistically speaking, the next Saviour will be from a different family." A hand raises,

"You have a question, Ms. Zelinski?"

Diana nods. "So can the Saviour be a boy?" I think by this point half of us realized we should've been writing this down because I along with six other classmates start scrambling to get out our notebooks and pencils.

Ms. Carvenon nods and responds "If a man decided to take estrogen supplements around the same time a Saviour dies or fulfills their duty, there is a chance that, theoretically, he could become the next Saviour. Although this has never happened before so we can't say for certain. There has however been a case of a Saviour who had been born with both male and female anatomy." The whole class marvels at this new information, our eyes twinkling with curiosity. For once, everyone has their eyes on our teacher rather than the blackboard to the side or the whiteboard to the front.

Ms. Carvenon continues "No one knows why Saviour's have to have more estrogen than testosterone, however it has been theorized that they may have been chosen by God as a way to equalize the playing field between men and women. Seeing as most spiritual leaders and speakers are men, it could be God's way of trying to say that women can be just as important. Although we will never know for sure." Now I'm not sure how to take notes 'cause I've never really learned how but I'm hoping my single word points will help me. Ms. Carvenon is talking kinda fast so it's hard to keep up. I look over at Anwen and her notes are super clear and pretty. I don't know how she does it.

"This theory came to be since Saviour's have always had Aether Magic. Many regard this magic as Holy Magic or magic that the angels use. And while Aether Magic is known as Anomaly Magic seeing as it is more of a skill set -like General Magic- only it gets passed down similarly to Genetic Magic. It has been seen to appear quite often in direct descendants of past Saviours. A prime example of this is the Chevalier family who are descended from the first Saviour, Alyssa Sawyer. Aether Magic is quite common in their family line. However, I want everyone to take this information with a grain of salt, it may soon change as most things do."

Alice raises her hand before speaking. "If the Chevalier family is directly descended from the First Saviour then why is their name 'Chevalier' and not 'Sawyer'?"

Ms. Carvenon calmly responds. "That's because Alyssa Sawyer had gotten married and changed her last name to Chevalier. So we should be referring to her as 'Alyssa Chevalier' however we call her by her maiden name due to her achievements being documented under her maiden name. The Chevalier family has produced more Aether Magic users than any other family, aside from the Saviour. Saviours are relatively easy to find despite this because only male descendants of past Saviours have been documented to be capable of wielding Aether Magic with the sole exception of Ceridwen Chevalier." I guess we all figured out that this is pretty important information because most of us scramble to write this all down.

~~~~~

After 2 hours of history and mathematics the lunch bell rings. My friends and I move our desks to sit by each other, golden eyes staring at my amethyst ones. "Diana? You're staring at me weird, what's up?"

Diana responds "Is it true that Saviour's remember things about their past lives?! I didn't realize Saviour history was so interesting until today. Is that why you read so much about it?" I pause, trying to remember what I read last year when I got into reading about the previous Saviour's. A confused look crosses my face.

"Yeah. um, as far as I know, Saviour's aren't past lives of each other, they're connected by the Aether. Whatever that means. Plus, we go to an Aetherist school, we don't believe in 'past lives.' Although Voidists believe that Saviour's do have past lives 'cause they believe in the cycle of reincarnation, I'd have to ask my father for more details since he was a theology major."
~~~~~

"I thought you knew all about Saviour history, I even thought you'd be the Saviour since you know so much." Catarina interjects, her amber eyes showing confusion.

I shake my head, "I don't have Aether Magic, remember? I mean yeah, it kinda glows but I don't think that exactly makes the cut. My Specialty Magic has to do with threads."

Anwen cocks her head to the side, "I could've sworn you did though..."

I shrug and start to eat my sandwich, "Does it matter? I mean even if I did have it, what difference does it make? It's not like I have to 'save the world' or whatever. The Nightmares haven't attacked any major cities since before we were born. We might even be able to form an alliance with them soon, if they don't wage war or anything, that is." As much as I should feel guilty for lying, I don't.

"True, but I also thought you had Aether Magic to be honest, or at the very least knew some healing spells..." Alice jumps in. I sigh and gently shake my head, my amethyst eyes meeting brown. Is Silvia glaring at me? She immediately smiles but something about that smile is off, like it isn't genuine. I shrug it off, it's probably nothing. Either that or Silvia's just tired, she did have a bit of a mad resting face after all. As my eyes start moving around, trying to see what's going on in class, I see Damon surrounded by our classmates. He's not doing much, if anything he's trying to ignore them. They're all asking questions and he's just...dryly answering. I cock my head to the side in confusion and my friends look in Damon's direction with me.

"He's pretty popular." I say in annoyance.

Anwen sighs, "I mean he's rich, comes from one of the most famous Reverie families in the world, and unfortunately, 'pretty' enough that Marion is after him." She makes a face of disgust and we, except for Silvia, start laughing.

~~~~~

Lunch ends and Ms Carvenon begins our next class "I hope you've all enjoyed your lunch because we're going to be learning about magic basics." I look around and notice we for the most part all brighten up at this news. We've been intensely excited about our training year classes also known as our 'Year 0.'

Damon scoffs, "Why should I be here when I'm already far more advanced than these half-wits."

Ms. Carvenon pinches the bridge of her nose and sternly says, "If you're so advanced, why do we use wands to use magi-"
~~~~~

"Maybe YOU use a wand, however I do not. wands are infant level tools to make a Reverie without skill appear better than they actually are. Using a wand is like admitting you still need training wheels to ride a bike. To put it simply, if you actually have skill you wouldn't even think of using such a tool. Tell me, do you also sleep with a stuffed bear and a night light?" We all stare at him with wide eyes. I look around more to see if everyone is as stunned as I am. Wait... holy smokes, Kaine. Is she really about to laugh right now? I mean, I guess she looks like she can contain it, but still! Everyone but Kaine is shocked into silence, did he REALLY just insult Ms. Carvenon? The most ruthless teacher at our school?

Our teacher's eyes narrow, "Bold words coming from a boy whose very existence is already on thin ice with the board."
I watch as Damon seethes, He looks like he's about to burst a blood vessel. Silvia's eyes shoot daggers at him, Wasn't she just planning on trying to get him to give her money? Wait...oh right, Silvia can't use magic without a wand. That must be why Kaine was laughing. Silvia kept talking about how she was gonna have Damon wrapped around her finger only for him to unknowingly destroy her ego. I continue to look around the room only to spot Kaine whose face is now flushing red, her hands covering her mouth as she desperately tries not to laugh.

"Kaine.... Don't make this worse by laughing...." I whisper under my breath. Ms Carvenon starts staring down Kaine.

"What exactly could you find funny about this situation Ms. Florence Guerrero?" It could've been the awkward silence in the room or the intense way the teacher is staring at her, but in the end Kaine began to convulse with laughter. She sighs, whether from annoyance or disappointment is unclear but what is clear is that the first day of our Reverie careers is not off to a good start.

Once Kaine finally calmed down she responded to the question with, "I'm sorry Miss I wasn't laughing at you. I was laughing because someone said something funny to me a while ago and I just remembered it now."

I guess that answer isn't the right one 'cause Ms. Carvenon starts writing extra math homework questions on the board, "Ms. Florence Guerrero, since class is so carefree, I'm sure you won't mind doing some extra questions for homework."

Chapter 8

The cool breeze flows through the air, the fatigue from our gym class the day prior is still killing me. I grimace as I kick a rock a little too hard in annoyance, I think back to how the rosy eyed boy, Damon Petrova, managed to outdo Mari in dodgeball. Everyone knows Marin Abdul is a force to be reckoned with, she is far stronger and faster than anyone in the grade. Yet somehow, Damon surpassed her easily. My eyes widen as said boy sits down on a rock adjacent to me and my friends, I sigh in annoyance. Damon sighs harder. Is this little shrimp trying to out sigh me?

I stand up and move in front of him, stepping into the sun, "Are you seriously trying to breathe more than me?!" My breathing accelerates, my friends giving me a look of confusion and bewilderment only for Damon to stand up, joining me in the sun. He scowls and accelerates his breathing too. Anwen looks at us on the verge of hyperventilating with disbelief, probably more disappointed at Damon since this is my regular off the cuff nonsense. We continue our breathing contest only for me to start wheezing and choking. Frick, I can't breathe! Am I seriously giving myself an asthma attack over Damon?! Catarina -my saviour- darts to my side and grabs my fanny pack so she can access my inhaler. She helps me use it. Alice rushes to get a teacher. Damon laughs, enjoying his victory only to start choking on air just as Ms. Carvenon arrives to take us inside. She holds a look of amazement but also disappointment at the scene before her. In her defence one of her students is sitting in the dirt heaving and taking her inhaler and the other is violently coughing.

She moves to us two and sighs, "It's the third day of school, do I really need to be calling your parents about this?"

Damon scowls "I will NOT be bested by that THING!" Ms. Carvenon sighs again and tells us to stay behind after school to see her. I shout, not wanting to get in trouble.

"No! We were just playing a game! A funny little game and it got out of hand!" My friends all look at me in surprise.

Just as Damon is about to respond, I continue, "Me and Damon are actually friends!" I chuckle awkwardly "Right, Damon?"

He obviously picks up on the cue but scowls, not caring to help me or himself as he says, "Like I'd be friends with an imbecile like you."

By this point, Ms Carvenon looks like she's about to give us infinite detentions.

Apparently that got Damon's attention 'cause he immediately quips, albeit a bit forcefully, "I wouldn't be merely friends with Amalia, we're best friends."

I sigh nervously and nudge Damon, I whisper "It's Emilia, not Amalia."

Damon whispers back "I don't remember caring. Just get us out of seeing her after school."

I move to hug Damon and happily chirp out, "Amalia is my um......middle name...? I can't believe you remembered that Damon!"

Ms. Carvenon nods, "I'm glad to see you two getting along then." She goes back into the air conditioned school while both of us sit in the dirt. The sunshine hits us at the perfect angle to make us overheat. Damon throws me off him the moment our teacher is out of sight. Rude.

"Never. Touch. Me. Again." He goes to another shady rock to sit on. Alice looks like she's about to go over and punch the living daylights out of Damon, however it is much too hot to get into unnecessary trouble seeing as it's the beginning of September in Toronto, Canada. Needless to say, while the weather is starting to cool down, it's still very hot.

Anwen sighs in disappointment. "I can't believe you gave yourself an asthma attack..."

I pout and cross my arms. "He was trying to beat me."

Alice adds "I'm more impressed that Damon actually went along with it."

I sigh, "Next week we have our general fitness test..." I groan to show my disdain and flop on the dirt, not caring if anything gets in my hair since the cool ground provides a great relief from the heat.

I continue "I'm gonna fail aren't I." While my words could be interpreted as a question, it's actually a statement. I know I'm going to fail the fitness test. I can't even walk up a small hill without getting winded, which in my defence, my lung function is at 46% on a good day. While I was never really bothered by the fact that I'm a cancer survivor, at times like this I curse the harsh treatment that destroyed my body. But I guess it's a pretty fair trade off considering I got to live, at least that's what I tell myself. It's not like I'll feel any different even if I was healthy.

Catarina sits on the cool dirt beside me, "Trust me, I'm not passing the test either. I'm not sure I even want to be a Reverie."

Diana walks up to us and adds "Yeah but you'd be making a lot of money."

"That's why I'm doing this." Catarina quips and laughs. I giggle at the notion that Catarina is willing to go to hell and back for some extra cash, it's not like she needed the money, she just wanted a high paying job.

Anwen rolls her eyes and smiles "At least you have magic, I got the short end of the stick."

"You have magic, I've seen you use it!" I exclaim.

Anwen crosses her arms, "My mana points is at 15, that's the only reason I'm in this class and not taking endurance and stamina training to enter the Academy. My resistance is high so that helps too. Unlike you and Catarina, I don't have Specialty Magic."

Me and Catarina look at each other, then at Diana and Alice, then back at Anwen before Diana says "You're still super talented you know? If Damon didn't have seemingly infinite knowledge, you'd be the smartest in the grade!" We all nod in agreement, having the utmost faith that Anwen could outsmart just about anyone.

"Either way, I'm sure we can all agree that all of us, except for Alice, are failing the fitness test next week." I pipe up and the others laugh, whether that be a real laugh or one of imminent doom is unknown. What is known is that we -save for Alice- aren't exactly known for being athletic.

Chapter 9

"Today's the day...I'm gonna die, aren't I?" I groan to show my displeasure, clutching my head as I prepare for my imminent demise. The school's gymnasium feels a lot less comfortable and a lot more dangerous.

I hear a scoff coming from behind me, great...Damon arrived. "If you are unable to do this much you should just drop out, or are you ashamed you'd be the first one?" Oh, so he's not even going to hide the fact that he's taunting me. I can play that game too.

I smile at him "I'm sure I'll be just fine, thank you for your concern." His expression contorts into one of annoyance, scoffing again before wandering off. I sigh in relief, noticing some of my friends enter the gym, and run towards them. Catarina and Diana look just as haggard as I do. Alice, as always, looks confident and prepared. This is her strong suit after all. As for Anwen, she just has her usual deadpan expression. Her crimson eyes and pale fawn skin, along with her sharper than usual canines gives everyone the impression that she's a vampire. The only thing "un-vampire-like" about her is that she has golden blonde hair. Which leads people to assume she's a vampire hybrid of sorts, they're right but they shouldn't treat her like an outsider for it.

The door to the gymnasium opens, causing us to all focus on her. Our teacher definitely commands respect, I'll say that. The lack of air conditioning in the gym causes it to get hotter as it gets closer to 9:00. Ms. Carvenon walks in with a tall, lanky middle aged man. His wavy chestnut hair and dim eyes are the first thing I notice. He looks...really sad. I smile, trying to make a good impression. Although I can't help but notice he looks like he's about to cry...He makes eye contact with me, looking like tears will fall from his eyes any second now...weirdo. I mean, I want to make a good impression but does no one else think it's kinda weird that he looks like he's about to start sobbing?

Ms. Carvenon speaks up. "Hello class, for today's fitness test you all have been granted a great honour of being taught by a former esteemed Reverie."

She turns to the man, "Would you like to introduce yourself to the children? All sixteen students are accounted for so don't worry about needing to repeat yourself for any latecomers."

The man smiles, it's a somber smile. When he looks at me and Damon, his smile becomes more genuine. Almost as if he's happy to see us specifically. He must have a couple screws loose if he's smiling at that jerk Damon Petrova. Also, why does he look like he's about to burst into tears every time he sees me? I get having a bad day but he's a former Reverie! Did they not let him reschedule this? I mean, being so sad you're about to break down in front of a bunch of kids seems like a pretty good reason to reschedule. Maybe it's capitalism? But Reveries are paid a lot, did he really spend that much? Maybe he has a gambling addiction or something. Ms. Belkin told us that addiction can happen to anybody. If that's the case, what a poor guy...

I snap out of my thoughts as the lanky man steps towards us, "Hello children, it's nice to meet you all. My name is Reynard and although I wouldn't call myself 'esteemed,' I was certainly a Reverie. I'll be watching over your bright minds while you all do your fitness test." Crap...right, our fitness test...yay...

Anwen raises her hand. "You said 'was' as if you're not currently a Reverie. Did you quit?"

Mr. Reynard smiles and says "Yes, I decided to retire so I could take care of my daughter, Aaliyah. She's about your age. Now, if there's no more questions, let's begin." He then splits us up into groups of five with one team getting a sixth person. I'm put with Alice, Catarina, Louis and Cameron... None of us are exactly good at sports, so safe to say we're the weakest team here. Alice is the only one of us with actual athletic talent. Even I can beat Louis in an arm wrestle, and that's sad...like, really sad, seeing as I can barely lift my fifteen pound dog. Cameron, on the other hand, is just as weak as me. Then there's me and Catarina who can't run because of our sorry excuses for lungs. We both have asthma but only I got the fancy sounding lung issue and lung scarring to top it off. A clap rings through the gym. Ms. Carvenon looks like she's about to tell us we're gonna be doing the beep test. Ugh I hate running.

She begins to speak "Mr. Reynard will be assessing your current capabilities by having you all do wind sprints." Sprints? Ok, that should be fine, I can run short distances...I just can't stop or the lack of oxygen or something will catch up to me or something, I don't know the science behind it. Ok I can do this. Mr. Reynard makes us line up in our groups in three straight lines.

He clears his throat, "The way this will work is the first person will run to the first line, bend down and touch it, then back. Repeat with the second line. At the third line clap the hand of the next person in line before sitting down at the end of your team's line." Kill me now...this is literally the beep test without the beep.

~~~~~

Our teachers give us a few minutes to talk amongst ourselves. I guess they're hoping we'll strategize since Reverie's often work in units or teams rather than alone. The one thing our teachers have overlooked is zero multiplied by one IS STILL ZERO. Alice is our only hope and she's more of a gymnast than a runner or a track star . Also it's not like Mari is on our team to help us either. I do a silent prayer. At this point I'm not doing this to win, I'm doing this to survive.
~~~~~

"Emilia, are you seriously praying?" Louis snickers.

"Of course I am!" I respond back, making sure he knows that I'm supposed to be annoyed. Alice tries to bring us all together as a team but it's not exactly working.

Cameron sighs "Well, it was nice knowing all of you." He salutes at us like a soldier going off to war.

Mr. Reynard smiles his sorrowful looking smile like a weirdo and hurries us into our lines. Our team doesn't care about what order we file in, it's not like we care about winning, it's all about survival. Cameron decides to go to the back of the line, leaving me the first one. Great, I'm first... if it weren't for the fact that I wanted to get this over with and go home, I would've felt the anticipation in the room. My senses heighten as I prepare myself for Mr. Reynard's whistle. If it weren't for my ears ringing I'd be able to hear the breathing of my classmates. The whistle goes off and I immediately bolt. I touch the first line and head back. I run to the second line and touch that one too, my lungs are burning, my breathing is accelerated. I think I'm gonna die. I can't get enough air. I run back and make it to the third line. My lungs hurt, are they supposed to hurt? I don't think they're supposed to hurt. I can't see anyone else and my vision is getting muddy but I touch the third line, barely managing to clap Alice's hand before booking it to the trash can where I dry heave. I can't hear anything past the throbbing heartbeat in my ears and everything's blurry. The next thing I know is I'm lying on the cold gymnasium floor, starfish style, as Ms. Carvenon snaps at me like they do babies when they chuck them into pools fully clothed.

My breathing is evening itself out and I notice my classmates are still running. Damon is screeching at his team to run faster. Everyone else is cheering. My team -needless to say- is coming in last since we have three people left to go. Everyone else is on their last runner. I sigh and sit up.

Mr. Reynard with his sad face asks "Are you feeling better? We thought you lost consciousness there for a bit."

I nod. "Oh uh, yeah I'm fine."

He smiles. "Here's a tip, when doing any kind of physical activity. Don't let your breathing get out of control, if you do that you'll be able to become a fine Reverie." I perk up, did he just say I'll become a "fine Reverie"? He seemed pretty certain, like he knows I'm pretty much guaranteed entry unless I do complete garbage this year, which, based on today, it seems like I'm not doing so well. Does he know I'm the Saviour? But...the Elder said that the only information that's getting revealed is that I've been found, not who I am. Maybe he's just being nice.

He smiles again and continues, "You have a bright future ahead of you, I'm sure you'll achieve many great things and be loved by your peers. Although you should make sure to make some enemies, that's the secret to Immortality." He beams at me. This guy is seriously strange. What's even weirder is that he knows my theory on immortality. Maybe he heard it from Cate, he probably went to his school to examine his class too. I smile back at him, finally, someone who's gets it. He might be weird but he's certainly less scary than Ms. Carvenon.

My team loses miserably, but it was fun seeing Damon get all worked up about his team's "lackluster performance." Although it wasn't as fun to see him do the sprints without even breaking a sweat. Show off... it's strange though... why IS he this athletic? I noticed it before during recess but he's surprisingly good at sports. He only came to this school this year which means he met his dad in the summer but that kind of greatness isn't something you can build up in 2 months... What the hell kind of childhood did he have?! Was his mom a sports buff or something? No, even die hard sports fans don't run their kid through the ringer like that... is his mom like a super crazy sports coach or something? Mr. Petrova is certainly an athletic man. I mean, he's a Reverie after all! His other kids are athletic too but this is seriously strange.

"Hey are you alright?" I'm brought back to the present to see Anwen standing in front of me.

Mr. Reynard and Ms. Carvenon go back to monitoring the class since I'm just resting, "Hey, Anwen? How strong is Damon?"

Anwen's expression turns into one of distaste "You're not gonna like the answer."

"Just say it."

"My dad estimates he can win in a fight against university level Reverie's in training. Probably even an actual Reverie." Right, Mr. Lupo is a teacher at the Academy so if anyone would know, it'd be him. My eyes widen.
Wait...a fight?

Curiosity hits me and I continue, "Fight? As in fisticuffs? I know you said he's apparently below average in mana control but to use his fists over magic?"

Anwen shakes her head. "Not fists. He uses weapons. Like swords, guns, and meteor hammers. He's a scary guy, I'd stay away from him if I were you. Not only is he a jerk but he's a level far above us in physical skill."

My jaw drops and I start whisper-yelling, "Who raised him?! Who in heck is giving a ten year old a sword, let alone any of the other things you listed?! Is his mom a psycho or something?!"

Anwen shrugs, "All I know is that his mom dumped him at his dad's this past summer, I'm not sure who she is though. She must be crazy though if she's giving her kid these weapons. He's super good at using them too, it's not like he's just learned how to wield them. He looks like he's been using them for years." We both sigh.

I decide to ask her another question, "Anwen? Is it just me or is Mr. Reynard like super weird?"

Anwen looks at me and nods "Trust me, I think we've all noticed it...well, I don't know if Cameron or Louis noticed since they're always off in their own world but it's pretty hard not to notice a tall man on the brink of tears."

I nod vigorously in agreement. "Do you think he's ok?"

"I don't know and I don't have enough energy to ask. It's hot and I'm tired." Anwen groans and flops down beside me on the cool floor. The floor is definitely filthy but she never did like the heat. We both look at each other lying on the floor and smile. Damon's frustrated ramblings can be heard in the background. The stale smell of the room is filling my nostrils along with the humid late summer air. I utter a silent prayer once more and say my thanks for my survival. As much as the beep test or wind sprints drained me dry, it was nice to take my first real step towards entering the Academy. It would be nice if I could take a picture of this very moment and keep it with me forever.

Chapter 10

It's finally Friday, the September air is getting cooler and it's the perfect day to go to the park with Cate. I haven't seen him since before school started. Truly a crime, I know. Now that school is done for the week, I can finally go see him again. I'm sure he won't hesitate to mention how nice the weather is. The fifteen to twenty-five degrees temperature range is his absolute favourite, although I'd be lying if I said it wasn't mine too. As the warm sun shines on my face, the cool breeze helps me feel better about not putting sunscreen on. After all, the sun can't burn me if the breeze cools me down before I cook, though I'm sure Cate will definitely explain to me otherwise, he's always been super smart like that. I just hope he doesn't tell my mom about it. As much as I should wear sunscreen so I don't get melanoma or something, I also don't want to hear another lecture about it. I know cancer is like a huge deal seeing as I beat it twice before. But in my defence, it's not like I'm choosing not to wear sunscreen, I just forget.

Regardless, I finally get to see Cate for the first time in over two weeks! The world has deprived me of Cate time, but now I get to see him again! His wavy chestnut hair, his freckles and his little beauty mark on the outer corner of his right eye, really add to his charm. At least that's what the adults say, they're always fawning over him. I think the silver streak in his hair near his right eye is super cool! People often think Cate's a girl, which to be fair, he's very pretty and he lets me put bows in his hair. I really like his eyes though, the royal blue colour to them gives off a mysterious look to him. Almost like he's an assassin or something, his general vibe on the other hand is anything but. He's always so nice, it's unfortunate that other kids like to pick on him. Although it has gotten better compared to two years ago. Actually, now that I'm thinking of it, Damon's eye colour doesn't suit him either. His rosy irises eyes don't exactly scream "force to be reckoned with" but his demeanour surely says otherwise. Cate would 100% look good with rosy eyes but Damon would still be a little brat regardless. Emphasis on the little. It's nice not being the shortest in the grade for once. I continue walking to the park when I see Mr. Reynard.

He still looks sad but I smile at him and he smiles back "Hello, Emilia. Where are you off to in such a hurry?" I smile, I'm glad he asked.

Any opportunity to talk about Cate is a great one "I'm going to see my friend, Cate!"

He smiles sombrely "I'm sure he's just as excited to see you as you are him. Be sure to value the life you have now and stick together." Ok...weird...that felt like a threat...is he threatening me? I smile awkwardly at him and we say our goodbyes as I continue to book it to the park. Although it's strange... How did Mr. Reynard know that

Cate's a boy? Did I say it wrong? No i definitely said Cate as in the girls name with a K...ARGH, now I'm second guessing myself! When I second guess myself I make mistakes, I should trust my instinct more! At least that's what Cate tells me. My forehead is starting to sweat from rushing what would normally be a ten minute walk. The breeze hitting me at just the right time, cooling my increasing body temperature, even if only a bit.

~~~~~

At last, the park enters my vision. I slow down, changing to a leisurely walk instead of the hurried pace I was going prior. The field looks like a sea of green, maybe I'll be able to find a four leaf clover somewhere. I get closer to the benches and picnic tables at the far end of the park, passing the play structures to my left. I dislike walking on grass or wood chips but going across the field is the quickest way to get to the picnic tables . They're crusty and look like they're gonna slide down the slight slope they're on but at least they're under some trees so there's shade. I look at the stupid looking frog rocker beside the play structures, it used to be a whale but Mari and another classmate broke it a year ago. They both got on it together and I guess the spring couldn't handle the weight, or it was old, probably both. Either way, it snapped and the park had to replace the whale with a frog. They somehow never got caught.
~~~~~

I arrive at the picnic tables and set my backpack down, the breeze feeling nice against my bixie cut. I used to have long hair, but then I got cancer. Unfortunately for me though, just as I got cured from one cancer the universe decided to give me a double whammy so I got another type. I survived that too, obviously. I remember how my long hair fell off in patches, my father wanted to shave it but I disagreed. I guess there's a certain allure to wanting to feel like a German Shepard in the spring. Having long hair was nice, but I also like feeling the breeze on my neck. As I wait for Cate, I notice a tall guy walk towards me. He looks familiar but I can't quite tell how I recognize him. His obsidian hair and copper eyes are very striking.

Once he gets close enough I ask him in a loud voice "Hello, do I know you?" He seems taken aback by how loud I was. The park isn't exactly empty after all.

He sighs and levels himself to my height. "My name is Aster Petrova. You're Damon's classmate, right?" I look at him with wide eyes. I saw him after the first day of school when Mr. Petrova made Damon 'apologize' to me.

"Oh" I laugh awkwardly. "I have a hearing loss so I didn't realize how loud I was being."

I try to give a convincing smile and he laughs "I see, so you know you were being loud then?" Uh oh...

He laughs again, I guess he noticed my 'I screwed up' expression 'cause he starts coughing from the laughter "You're one smart cookie, you know that?" My eyes widen. Did a member of the Petrova family...just compliment me...?

Aster continues "Damon was complaining about how there's a 'severe lack of intelligent life' in his class, so I was worried that next year's newest Reverie's in training wouldn't be up to par."

He smiles reassuringly, "But now? Now I think that my little brother couldn't be more wrong. Most kids wouldn't be so cautious, I mean this is a safe neighbourhood after all. You on the other hand analyzed the situation and made sure to bring attention to us. You're vigilant, you'll make a fine Reverie."

He puts his hand out, I shake it and smile "Thank you." His eyes widen, as if he's surprised that I thanked him.

He sighs "Why couldn't you be my younger sibling instead?"

"Wait, why aren't you at the academy?" I tilt my head in confusion.

He makes a face that tells me he's done something bad, "Well, I burned my classmates' herbs in herbology class and the teachers got mad so my whole class got sent home for a week."

"Millie!" I turn my head to see Cate rushing towards me. I beam at him and get up from the crusty picnic table. I wave my arm above my head to signal him, as if he couldn't already see me.

Aster smiles. "I see your friend is here, have fun!" I nod at him, still beaming, he walks away.

Once he gets close enough to me, he flashes a knowing smile, "Did you put sunscreen on this morning?"

I put on a nervous looking smile, "Well...you see...the thing is..."

I pause, he's still smiling at me, might as well go down with confidence "The sun can't burn me if the wind cools me down before I cook!"

He takes in the information and pauses before going into a ramble, "Actually, the wind can lessen your skin's natural defences against the sun, which will allow more UV rays to enter and harm you. The wind most likely affects the skin by it being a direct irritant that leads to the shedding of the skin's outermost layers, which makes the freshly exposed skin more susceptible to UV radiation damage."

He puts his bag down and grabs a bottle of sunscreen. "Even short exposure to two primary UV radiation kinds can harm your skin's DNA."

He applies thick globs of the sunscreen onto his hands before applying it to my face in lines resembling makeup techniques, "UVB rays cause sunburn, while UVA rays produce tanning, wrinkles, and skin aging. Damage from both or any kinds of rays builds up over time, causing DNA changes that may result in skin cancer."

He smiles and rummages through his bag down before grabbing a spray can of sunscreen "I knew you were going to forget so I brought two different kinds for you." He gives me the spray can and watches intensely as I rub the sun screen he applied on my face in as well as spray on the sunscreen. Once it's on he hugs me.

As I hug back I ask "Have your classmates been mean to you again?" He pauses, then nods.

I continue "It's not as bad as two years ago though, right?" He nods again.

"Good" I respond then break from the hug.

"You'll tell me if they're doing anything really bad right?" He nods once more. I sit down on the bench of the crusty picnic table.

I continue "You know, you could always just beat them up. You can tell your parents that I told you to do it."

Cate stays silent for a second then says, "But if I do that, the chances of me entering Reverie Academy will decrease by at least fifty percent."

I look up at him and smile brightly to show support "I knew you'd be chosen to potentially enter Reverie Academy! You're super smart and you're super talented too!"

Dim bursts of light flicker around us, like little fireworks. Except you can actually see these ones in the afternoon light, "My cousin, Rowan is also eligible. I'm so excited that all my favourite people might be together in one place!"

As Cate marvels at the flickers of dimming light, I add, "Congratulations on being selected as a candidate for Reverie Academy! Sorry I can't put on more of a show for you, my magic has been a bit wonky recently."

I laugh awkwardly then continue "Promise me we'll both get in?" I hold out my pinky.

Cate smiles before saying "Well actually, the odds that we both get in are really slim. There are many cases in which none of the prospective children chosen at the beginning of the year get a lucid crystal by the end of it. In fact, the average year size for this year should amount to about one hundred forty-five thousand, three hundred seventy-nine. Which may seem like a high number until you remember that Reverie Academy has grade thirteen and offers graduate school."

I guess Cate noticed my deadpan expression 'cause he sighs and links his pinky with mine, "Ok ok, I promise we'll both enter Reverie Academy."

I smile brightly at him and he smiles back, "Anyways, What is new with you?"

I sit down on the bench before looking up in thought, I respond, "We had this retired Reverie come to my school, I don't really know what for since he just kinda watched us. He knew my theory on immortality so he's definitely cool. You told him about it, right?"

Cate laughs, "Millie, correlation does not equal causation and no, I haven't told anyone."

I stare at him blankly, "Those are big words."

"Just because things align doesn't mean they're related." He smiles back at me.

If Cate didn't tell Mr. Reynard, then who did? I groan and rapidly lean back, hitting my back on the picnic table. "OW!" I sit back up and try to clutch at my back in an attempt to soothe my pain. That traitorous intellectual, Cate starts laughing at my misery. His royal blue eyes welling up with tears from how hard he's laughing.

"Millie?"
 He manages to gasp out as his laughter subsides, "Are you ok?"

I whine and flop onto the dirt and start shifting my weight across my back in an attempt to stop the throbbing, "It hurtsssss."

He gets off the bench and lays beside me in the dirt, we look up at the green leaves on the tree. "You can hit me for laughing."

I shake my head, "I'm not gonna hit you. I already made your parents upset when I cut your hair that one time. Which, in my defence, you weren't gonna get that gum out any other way."

"I remember that."
He nods, "To be fair, you let me cut your hair to make it even."

I turn my head to stare at him whilst grinning, "You didn't do it though, you said you'd cut my hair once I actually had hair to cut."

He laughs, "I'm still not gonna cut your hair, my mom would be so mad if I did. She says your hair is nice and healthy now that you actually have some." He sits up and ruffles his hair to get the dirt out.

I sit up and stare at the leaves, "Once we're at the Academy, we should form a team. We'd be unstoppable."

We beam at each other before he responds, "We'll be the best team."

~~~~~
~~~~~

As the hours pass by, our time at the park comes to an end. Cate plucks a hair from his head, turning it into a jellyfish. I've gotten pretty used to identifying jellyfish since I've met him.

The mushroom-like appearance of the small jellyfish floating near me is truly adorable, "Is this a cannonball jelly?"

He nods and responds "It's not much but it'll keep you safe on your way home. The chances of someone messing with a magical floating jellyfish is pretty slim." We wave goodbye and I walk back to school where my mom is picking me up. Cate lives pretty close by so he has no trouble getting home. His Speciality Magic has to do with jellyfish, it's really cute. I turn around to see if he's gone. I smile when I notice he turns to look at me too. I wave my arm above my head and he copies me, his hair slightly glowing as the sun sets. Ah, the joys of having bioluminescent hair. I poke the jellyfish floating near my head and it jiggles. As I turn back around, I notice someone looking at us from the trees. I should be scared but both me and Cate are far enough that nothing will happen. That person is probably playing with their kids, so why does something feel off?

"He's staring at you specifically, you're in danger." I sigh as the shadowy figure follows me. She always follows me so I don't know what I expected. I brush off her warning and the feeling in my gut that something is wrong, continuing to walk back to the school.

"Emilia?" a voice comes from behind me as I'm walking down John Street.

I turn around, "Alice! Hi!"

She runs up to me and we start walking together, "You were with Cato at the park just now, right?" I nod.
"Were you able to get your results from a week ago?"

Crap, I should probably be honest but I can't, "Nope, I would've thought I'd get mine by now but I guess they forgot." We continue walking down John Street, cars and people passing us.

"That's so weird. I didn't think they'd just forget like that." she says. I shrug. We get to the crosswalk and we wave goodbye. Hopefully Cate made it home ok.

Chapter 11

Another week has passed by, sorta. I mean it's Thursday so we're basically done the week. It's been six days since I've seen Cate, how tragic. Well, if he's gonna be a Reverie then he should try to stand up for himself a bit. Hopefully his teacher catches his bullies in the act so they'll be dropped from the potential academy candidates list.

"Emilia? You ok?" I blink and I'm brought back to the present. Alice is looking at me, slight concern etched in her features.

"Oh, yeah. Sorry, I'm fine. I just zoned out." The noise of the classroom filling my ears.

"She was probably thinking about Cato." Anwen says teasingly, laughing directly afterwards.

Catarina places her elbows on the desk and rests her chin on her hands. "Anwen, that's mean!" She turns to me then whispers something. I smile back graciously, not wanting to be annoying by asking her to repeat herself since I didn't hear what she said. I look around the classroom. Damon is near the door, Max, Aaron and Lila are with him, as always.

I turn to Anwen, swallowing the piece of sandwich I was eating before responding, "He's my friend, it's not like I have a crush on him or anything."

Alice raises her eyebrow, "I thought you did to be honest. You talk about him a lot." Diana, Catarina and Anwen nod in agreement. Silvia stays quiet.

I stay silent, in thought before responding, "He's someone weaker than me. I'm taking responsibility for him by protecting him. It's not like he's capable of protecting himself, at least not yet anyways. He just needs some help right now but one day he'll definitely be able to fend for himse-"

"We have our general magic test today and you're worried about your weak ass friend?" Of course... I know Silvia is brash but she's never called someone-... No she has. I don't know what exactly I expected from her to be honest. Me and the others stare at her with shock in our eyes.

"What? I'm just saying, why should I care about Emilia's pathetic friend? If he can't defend himself he might as well kill himself before he dies a brutal death from a Nightmare."

"Silvia! That's going too far!" I exclaim, although not loud enough for our other classmates to bother to look over at us.

She rolls her eyes, "It's called advice, learn to take it, Emilia. Someone like that is bound to bring shame to his family. I don't know how you can stand to protect someone like tha-"

"Silvia, you've said enough." We both turn to Anwen. She looks angry. She starts speaking sternly.She NEVER speaks sternly, "Just because you're salty that Damon's been a jerk to you doesn't give you the right to say things like that. Especially since you don't have Specialty Magic and Cato does. By that logic he's far more likely to succeed than you are, so stop goading Emilia."

Silvia's face scrunches up in anger as she slams her hands on the desk, "You don't have Specialty Magic either! Neither does Diana or Alice! If anything, you'll be the one to drop out with your measly fifteen manapoints!"

Anwen's eyes narrow and she sighs in annoyance "Ok and? Unlike you I have good grades and I don't taunt people till they snap and then cry wolf when they rightfully react to your antagonism. Not to mention my mana control is much better than yours, and unlike you, I don't need -what did Damon call them?- an 'infant level tool to make a Reverie without skill appear better than they actually are.' So who's really the one least likely to succeed, huh, Silvia? Can you do anything other than basic elemental magic? I heard Kaine's even teaching you fire magic yet you can't do that properly either." Cameron and Louis who are sitting in the group of desks behind us, start cackling. I guess they heard what Anwen said. Silvia seethes before getting up and flipping us off. She walks over to Kaine, clearly upset and starts loudly crap talking us. Typical. The bell rings, signalling the end of lunch. We all eagerly pack away our food. It's the day of our general magic test after all. I wonder if Mr. Reynard is coming to teach us today. I mean, he didn't really do much last time.

Maybe he came to give professional insight to Ms. Carvenon. Like as an estimate as to how many of us will make it. "Children, hurry and get in line. I'm sure you're all eagerly awaiting to get started." We all rush into a very sloppy line at the instruction of our scary but also surprisingly nice teacher. She sighs in annoyance, probably 'cause the line we made looks more like a squiggle than a line.

"Is this a line?" We start hustling into a straighter line, not wanting to hear another speech about how the kindergarteners are outdoing us in 'orderly conduct' as Damon calls it. Once our line is deemed as acceptable by Ms. Carvenon's standards she leads us down the stairs, past Ms. Akt's class and towards the school yard. We pass Mr. Crowbak's class too. Mari waves at the older kids sitting in math class. Once we get to the yard, she splits us into pairs. Lucky for me, I get paired with Anwen. A wonderful choice since we're both good at mana control. The chances of me and Anwen destroying the school is 0. Though I feel kinda bad since we're pretty much on opposite ends of the magic spectrum. I look around to see all the other pairs. Yeah, we got this. The only people here that're even decent at water magic are Mari and Marion, and they're not paired together. Ms. Carvenon leads all the pairs to different parts of the yard. A chain link fence keeps us from running away. A weird thing to say but it's happened before.

"I wonder what the test is gonna be like." I wonder out loud.

Anwen responds "My big sister Anastasia told me during her candidate year, that the general magic test was based on mana control rather than a show of power. It probably hasn't changed since I doubt the city wants to pay for damages caused by rookie academy candidates." That definitely makes sense. Anwen has always been really smart. She is a Lupo after all. It's only natural that her family is super dependable, they're related to the seventh Saviour. I think Zinnia Lupo is like Anwen's great aunt or great great aunt. Something like that. We watch Ms. Carvenon arrange the other pairs.

"What's it like being related to the most talented Saviour in history?" I ask.

Anwen looks up in thought before responding, "Being related to Zinnia would probably be really great if I were Anastasia. People hear my last name and assume I'm super impressive like Zinnia when I don't even have Specialty Magic. Anastasia on the other hand is at the top of her class in everything, she's what people expect from someone related to a Saviour." My eyes widen. I think I accidentally hit a sore spot...

I guess Anwen figures out I'm feeling bad about this so she continues, "I mean, it's not like I particularly hate my position or anything. My goal right now is to surpass Damon and take back my spot as top of the class." We both laugh.

Ms. Carvenon starts to speak, "Once you and your partner are ready, you'll be using water elemental magic for this. To those of you who have Specialty Magic or are more adept at other forms of General Magic, you're going to need to learn how to adapt to your surroundings so think of this as an extra challenge for you." Alright, this doesn't sound as easy as I thought it'd be but that's ok! My mana control is definitely above average with how much I practice. Although water magic isn't exactly easy, it's definitely better than fire. It feels slippery, like a bar of soap when you move it, fire magic is more stable but definitely more dangerous. I guess they're both hard since they're both hard to control but at least there's no chance we'll burn each other. Me and Anwen smile and give each other a thumbs up.

Ms. Carvenon clears her throat. "You'll be using these." She holds up a giant bucket of water balloons, they look overfilled, like even touching them will make them burst.

"Your goal is to avoid getting wet. Whichever of you is the driest by the end gets to skip any one test." Oh, lovely. I give Anwen my best 'I thought you said it'd be a mana control test' look. She shrugs and gives me a 'I said it was PROBABLY a mana control test' look. We both sigh.

Anwen looks up in realization. "Wait... the goal is to stay dry right?" I nod. She gets closer to me and continues in a quieter voice.

"The assumption she's probably making is that we'll end up turning on each other. Those balloons are filled so that if we're not careful, they'll burst." I nod again. I thought that much was obvious.

She smiles "Reverie's hardly ever work solo, they work as a team. We don't necessarily need the balloon. This test is about water, not the balloon." The other groups start getting their water balloons and popping them on each other.

My eyes widen in realization. "We just need to pop the balloon and then pass the water between each other. There's no way we'll be punished for being dry because this test is about precision AND teamwork." Anwen nods and smiles her signature maniacal grin. Her lips curling upward, showing her teeth. She really does have the creepiest smile, although that's definitely not a bad thing.

"Are you girls going to get a balloon?" We look at our teacher and nod. Anwen carefully grabs a balloon. We look around and notice that all our classmates are at least a little wet. The concrete beneath our feet looking splotchy from all the popped balloons.

Anwen's smile gets larger, "You ready, Emilia?" I nod and she tosses the balloon in the air. I use my Aether Magic to create densely packed yet dimly lit light before darting up to prick the balloon. The water starts falling and I close my eyes in preparation to get wet. It's not like I don't trust Anwen but water magic is very smooth. It's like butter melting on a hot pan. The water doesn't hit me. I hear Anwen laughing. I open my eyes and see her playing with the water in the air.

"I thought you were ready." She teases. I grin and pull the water towards me, my heart skips a beat as it darts towards me. I guess I used too much force. Me and Anwen just start passing the water between each other. Ms. Carvenon's face is filled with shock. It seems like she wasn't expecting us to work together. As she turns her back to us, I feel something hit me from behind. My back is wet.

I turn around only to see Silvia who's laughing, "Sorry, Emilia! Looks like I'm a bit clumsy." Are you kidding me? She can't even use magic without a wand let alone water magic. The rubber of the balloon is on the ground in front of me. She fricken threw that at me! I hear a splash of water come from behind me again.

I turn back to see Anwen who's equally wet, "I'm sure Silvia didn't mean to get you wet, Emilia. I mean, not all of us can be good at water magic. Look at me and Damon." Anwen points to Damon and Max who are completely drenched. Damon looking absolutely livid.

"Even we're bad at controlling water. We all have room for improvement, some more than others." She flashes her signature creepy smile.

Our teacher clears her throat. "Since you're all soaking wet you can go to the office and they'll dry you off. Once you've done that you can grab your backpacks and head home. I'm dismissing class early today." All our faces light up, well, except Damon's. His face is in a permanent scowl. Anwen nudges me towards the door and we both start walking to the office.

~~~~~

Once I'm dry, I head back to class to grab my backpack. As much as I hate climbing six flights of stairs, it's arguably better than being trapped in that death box elevator. At least the stairs will only kill me internally. The elevator is so slow and rickety, I'm surprised no one's died in it. First flight, I hate this. Second flight, kill me now. Third flight, screw it, I'll run the rest. Fourth flight, I regret doing that SO much. Fifth flight, I'm going to die. Sixth flight, I finally get to the top. I collapse onto the floor face down, my cheek touching the cool probably tiled floor. I don't know what type of floor I'm laying on, and frankly I don't care. It's probably riddled with germs either way but it's cooling me down from going up all those stairs. I heave and slowly get back on my feet. Trudging towards my class so I can grab my backpack. I pass by Ms. Belkin's class and Ms. Octinera's class, finally making it to my class. Most of the backpacks are gone from what I can see. The cubby area is slightly obstructed by Ms. Carvenon's desk and filing cabinets. I enter the classroom and walk left to my cubby. Only five bags are left counting mine. I grab my bag and start walking back down the six flights of stairs. The trip down is obviously much easier than the trip up.
~~~~~

"Emilia, wait up!" Alice yells. I stop walking to let Alice catch up with me. She yelps as she trips down three of the steps. She's completely soaked from head to toe.

"Wait, how are you all dry?"

I tilt my head, "Ms. Carvenon told us to go to the office to dry up, remember?"

"Ohh, that makes sense. I went to the washroom and when I got back, everyone was gone." She groans.

"I can't believe you guys left without me." We both laugh. We reach the bottom of the steps and I see my mom. I guess the school called her to pick me up. I wave 'goodbye' to Alice and we go our separate ways.

I walk towards her and say, "Hi, mom."

She smiles lovingly at me, "How was your day, Emilia?"

"It was good!" I respond. She takes my backpack from me and we head to the car. Passing the office. We walk down the hall towards the gymnasium. Passing by all the graduate photos and climbing 5 steps. Once we pass another few classrooms and the gymnasium we enter the yard, walking towards the gate before unlatching it. We get to the car and drive home.

Chapter 12

Once we pack up our lunches, Ms. Carvenon walks up to the front of the classroom. "Today, children, is the day you have your first try at sparring with each other." Lovely, we love that. This is gonna be great. I am totally 100% amazing at physical activity. I definitely didn't clock out when Mr. Reynard came to class. Definitely not.

"We will go down to the gymnasium -with your bags- and you'll be put into pairs. You'll then have to subdue your partner. Needless to say you will not be allowed to bite your partner." Cameron and Louis visibly deflate. Seems like they were planning on biting their way to victory.

"I will give you a number between one to eight and your partner will be the one with the matching number." As she starts numbering us off, I begin looking around to see who's partnered with who. We're lined up against the chalkboard like when we play pamplemousse. I look outside the windows across the room to see the staff parking lot, or, at least the fence that encloses the parking lot. Ms. Carvenon comes up to me and labels me as eight.

"You are partnered with Catarina." The sigh of relief I just let out clearly got my teacher's attention cause she chuckles.

I hear another voice laugh, "As if you're going to get any real experience sparring with someone like her, though I suppose with how weak you are, any progress is good progress." Great. I thought she'd stay quiet today. The perks of having a shadow woman follow you is truly an experience. I sigh and ignore her.

Catarina comes up and smiles at me "I'm glad it's you."

I laugh and nod "Yeah, same. I was hoping I wouldn't get paired with Max or Silvia."

She looks at me, confusion evident in her features "Why? Max seems nice." Our teacher starts guiding us down the stairs. We pass Ms. Akt's class rather than Ms. Belkin's and Ms. Octinera's class.

"He's a year older than us and he's an athlete. He's way bigger and stronger than me and as nice as he is, I like living." I respond and Catarina giggles at my dramatics.

"Well I'm sure Max wouldn't body slam you or anything."Catarina quips back. I shudder at the thought of being body slammed. I mean, that seems like it would hurt a lot. We walk down some more stairs and past Mr. Crowbak's class and turn left towards the entrance of the gym.

Ms. Carvenon begins to place us around the space, leaving big enough gaps so that we don't crash into each other. Me and Catarina are in the top corner by the other exit. Not the exit from the rest of the school to the gym, the exit from the gym to the yard. Me and Catarina look at each other, unsure of what exactly to do. "Alright, class. Your goal is to get your opponent off their feet. You get one point for every time you knock your partner down. You will be keeping track of your own points. The top 3 of you with the most points get to leave school early tomorrow." Now that's definitely a way to get us to turn on each other.

She continues, "Once you and your partner feel you've done enough, you may sit on the stage and watch the rest of the class." I look at my partner and she gives me a thumbs up. We're good. Ms. Carvenon tells us that we're free to begin. A loud thud echoes around the room. Me and Catarina turn our heads to see Damon standing above Silvia. Her brown eyes glaring daggers into his rose coloured ones. Did he just... throw her on the floor? Anwen was right, Damon is a force to be reckoned with. I stare at Silvia with wide eyes, that could've been me. Silvia gets up and rushes to punch Damon. She has her fists up like a boxer, trying to show off her apparent boxing skills to which she has none. I guess Damon somehow figured that out though 'cause he scoffs and pulls her close with his right hand before putting his left on her face and shoving her down. The room goes silent. Everyone looks shocked except for Ms. Carvenon who apparently left the gym, probably to get her water. Even Aaron who's normally cocky is standing with his mouth agape.

I whisper to Catarina, "Whatever god allowed us to escape being paired with him is truly generous."

She nods vigorously and smiles reassuringly, her amber eyes staring at me softly. "I guess we should try to get started?" I agree with her and we both do this awkward shimmy type movement, not knowing what exactly to do to not hurt each other. Our classmates all go back to sparring with each other. All of us are clearly struggling, save for Damon.

I try to show optimism by saying, "Let's just go for it, no hard feelings." My partner agrees and hesitantly comes towards me. Despite her being taller than me I'm not afraid. Catarina would never hurt a fly.

She points behind me, "Look out!" She exclaims. I turn to look behind me. I'm on the floor. I cannot believe I just fell for that.

Catarina who's standing above me with an apologetic look on her face, "I'm sorry. I didn't think you'd fall for that." She grimaces and extends her hand to help me back up. I take her hand and yank her down to the ground. She looks at me with surprise on her face, though it only lasts a second. I stare at her with a wide grin. She smiles back and laughs. We decide to continue sitting on the ground. We both know that neither of us will be in the top three and we already showcased something.

Catarina leans over to me, "Do you think we should go on the stage to watch? So we don't end up in someone's way or anything."

"Oh, yeah. That's a good idea." We walk close to the gym walls and make our way to the steps that lead to the stage. Once we get on the stage we sit down on the ledge, watching our classmates do far better than we did. Mari is paired up with Kaine and they seem like equal opponents for each other. She's taller than Kaine and definitely has the upper hand however Kaine likes to play dirty. Although she should've put her deep black hair in a bun instead of her regular high pigtails, maybe Kaine knows that Mari wouldn't yank her hair to score a point? Can't say Kaine would do the same for Mari though, if we were outside she would've thrown dirt in her eyes by now. Me and my partner both look at Silvia and Damon upon hearing Silvia's haggard breathing. She's definitely not happy. Though she was trying to show off before, she's just trying to get at least one hit in by now.

I turn to Catarina, "I kinda feel bad for her."

"Don't, if she gets hurt for real, that's only because she's too prideful to admit she's lost. She's only still fighting because she doesn't want to acknowledge that she's not the strongest in the class." I nod, agreeing with her. Although it's kind of embarrassing to see Silvia lose this badly. Even Max and Aaron are more equally matched and Aaron is losing by a long shot. While both Aaron and Max play volleyball for the school, Max is in the grade above us and he's a lot bigger than Aaron so he's able to overpower him pretty easily. Kaine goes to grab Mari's beach blonde curly hair but lucky for her, it's in a high bun. She twists Kaine's arm and knocks her to the ground. Mari is definitely a force to be reckoned with, even if she has no experience fighting. Which to be fair, I don't think any of us do, except for Damon apparently.

Catarina points at Kala and Louis, "I heard from Louis that he and Kala are cousins. They share a great grandma or something like that. Since Kala is the tallest in the class, I would've never guessed they were related."

I hum in response, "It's a little funny watching Louis try to get a punch in -or whatever he's trying to do- while Kala just needs to extend her arms to stop him. Although it's good no one's successfully pulled any hair yet."

Catarina nods eagerly, "I was just about to say that! Louis's hair is so pretty! It's such a nice medium brown colour. I wish my hair was that nice." We continue watching as Kala's palm is on Louis's forehead and Louis is unsuccessful trying his best to get a hit in.

My eyes narrow as I turn to her, "Your hair is so nice! It's so fluffy and soft."

"Thanks, Emilia." She responds in a soft voice.

After watching Louis continue to not even manage to graze Kala, I ask, "Hey, Catarina? Who do you think is gonna make it to the Lucid Ceremony at the end of the year?"

She looks up in thought, "Marin and Damon for sure. They're too talented not to make it. You, Anwen and Max most likely will too."

"What about you? Do you think you'll make it?"

"Maybe, I have Specialty Magic but I'm not really sure. Probably not since I don't think I'm strong enough for the job." She laughs awkwardly.

I groan, "You can literally transfer parts of your soul into objects and control them like you control your own body. I think you'll definitely make it to the Lucid Ceremony." Catarina smiles softly, she opens her mouth to talk but gets interrupted by Silvia letting out a pained yelp. Ms. Carvenon rushes towards Damon.

He scoffs, "Beek charged towards me, attempting to incapacitate me by reaching for my eyes. I was merely practicing self defence. If anyone is going to be chastised it should be that vengeful wretch."

Marion, ever the ally of justice, speaks out, "It's true Miss, Silvia tried to go for his eyes." Honestly I can't tell if Marion's doing this because she feels it's the right thing to do or if it's because she has a crush on Damon. I did hear her talk about her wish for Damon to talk to her but I don't know. It doesn't matter to me either way. Although it is nice to see Silvia's violent personality come to light in front of a teacher.

Our teacher sighs, "Very well then. Silvia, come with me to the office. I understand this exercise is exciting and I didn't specify 'no gouging out eyes' however please make note to not do that again." She helps Silvia up and takes her to the office. Once she leaves the gym the class erupts with noise.

"Wait what happened?"

"Is Silvia ok?"

"How did she even get hurt? She seemed fine." As the chatter fills the gym, Anwen, Diana and Alice join me and Catarina on the stage. Anwen and Diana look tired while Alice looks as energetic as ever

"I got paired up with Lila." Anwen groans. I tilt my head in confusion. Isn't that a good thing?
"She's surprisingly strong, athletic too." She says as if reading my mind.
We all share our condolences before Anwen speaks again, "You and Catarina looked like you had fun."

Catarina smiles and we fist bump each other, "Heck yeah we did."

Diana groans, "Me and Alice got paired together..."

Alice gasps in mock offence, "I am a delightful sparring partner."

"Tell that to my back! You flung me left, right and centre!" Exclaims Diana. Me and Catarina attempt to stifle our laughter.

"It's not funny, guys!"

"Since you all seem to be having such a good time I'm sure you won't mind doing some laps around the north yard." I, along with my other classmates, all shut up, not wanting Ms. Carvenon to unleash her wrath upon us.

"Oh, so you do know how to be quiet. Very well then. Get in a line and tell me your score, NOT your partner's score." We line up and one by one, tell her our score and sit by the wall once we've done so. Once it's my turn I use my most confident voice and I tell her that I have a grand total of 1 point. She raises an eyebrow then sends me to the wall most of the class that already told her their scores. Catarina tells her her score. Ms. Carvenon closes her eyes and inhales through her nose, most definitely realizing we did zero work. Regardless, she sends Catarina over to the wall where I'm sitting. I'm sure Miss isn't too thrilled that we're in a giant clump rather than side by side or in rows but I don't think she's getting paid enough to care. At least that's what Oppa said about most teachers.

"Do you think she realized we pretty much did nothing?" Catarina murmurs.

I raise my eyebrows and give her a deadpan stare, "Take a wild guess."

"How many points did you guys get?" Alice comes to join us by the wall.

Me and Catarina both say "One." simultaneously.

Alice's mouth makes an 'O' shape, seemingly understanding why Ms. Carvenon was irritated, "I got seven and Diana got two. Between us, I felt bad so I let her get those points in. Don't tell her though."

Anwen and Diana join us, "What're you guys talking abou-"

"Alright children, I will announce the top three students with the most points." As our teacher talks, Anwen moves to sit beside Catarina while Diana sits between me and Alice.

"In first place, Damon Petrova w-" The class groans but quiets down the second Ms. Carvenon gives us her legendary stern stare that we've all heard rumours about.

"As I was saying, Damon Petrova is in first place with 30 points." Holy crap. I can hear the murmuring of my classmates, saying things like

"Good thing I'm not Silvia." and
"Silvia held her own against Damon?" Silvia even had the height advantage over him since she's much taller than me and I'm like a quarter ruler taller than Damon. He must've been going easy on Silvia... like, really easy. Just how strong are Reverie's anyways? How strong are Nightmares?

I'm jolted out of my thoughts by our teacher continuing, "In second place, Marin Abdul with 17 points." I reach over to tap Mari on the shoulder, she's beaming with pride.

"Congratulations Mari." I whisper back at her, my smile equally warm.

"In third place, Max Brandt with 13 points."

A familiar voice echoes from behind me, "You know, if you actually tried, you could kill everyone here." And here I thought she'd leave me alone today. I may not be able to see her standing behind me but I can feel her presence, the shadowy woman that always follows me.

"I told you, there's a price for your existence. How much longer are you going to make me wait for my payment?" I let out a soft sigh and continue to ignore her.

"If it weren't for me you'd be dead!" She exclaims.

Max turns to look at me, I make eye contact with him and put on my best smile, mouthing 'Good job' to him.

He mouths back a 'thanks' before turning back to face the teacher. I like Max, he's nice, he has this nostalgic vibe to him. I can't place my finger on why though. Something about him seems familiar. Just as the class is about to get up, Ms. Carvenon clears her throat,

"Because I'm feeling kind today I have one more person to announce, an honourable mention, if you will. This person will get any singular piece of candy from Ms. Belkin's candy box." Our eyes dart to our wonderful, gracious and generous teacher.

"Our honourable mention is Kaine Florence Guerrero with 12 points. You're all dismissed."

She turns to Kaine, "You can pick up your candy tomorrow or Friday during lunch." My classmates truly are on a whole other level.

The shadow woman puts her hands on my shoulders and speaks in my ear, "You should fulfill your end of the deal while you still have Aether Magic. Will people really accept you if they know you have Void Magic?" Me and the rest of the class start getting up. Somehow

I'm not surprised I have Void Magic... This might as well be happening.

Chapter 13

Anti Peace

"Ugh, finally." I turn my head to look at Anwen who's walking my way.

"October is here at last. No more heatwaves." I laugh and she continues walking before stopping in front of me.

"It's been October since Saturday, ya know?" I respond.

Anwen grimaces, "Saturday was literally boiling, I stayed inside all day." We look around the south yard and watch as all the younger kids start pouring in. Most of them heading towards the play structure beside us. Being the oldest in the yard meant kids looked up to us. Not that there's not much to look up to in my case.

I look up in thought, having something I want to say but forgetting what it is. Ah, right, "Hey, by the way. What exactly happened to Silvia on Wednesday? She hasn't been at school since Damon injured her."

Anwen scoffs, "Injured? Oh please. The 'injury' is a sore finger. Her mom thought Damon broke it so she took Silvia to the ER only for it to not even be sprained. Nothing happened. Nothing was out of place. Chances are, Silvia was just overreacting and wanted to get

Damon in trouble." Seriously? A sore finger? With how loud she yelped I would've thought he broke it in multiple places.

Anwen continues, "Damon went easy on her, he even beat Anastasia in a sparring match." My face contorts into an expression of disbelief. I know Anwen said he's super strong but to hear that someone I actually know got beat by him definitely gives me a better idea of how strong this guy really is. I mean, Anastasia is a fourth year but she already has full fledged Reverie's vying for her to join their team once she graduates.

"Do you think she'll come to school today?" I ask almost hesitantly. More kids start to flood the school yard.

Anwen rolls her eyes, "If she doesn't then she's definitely milking the 'injury' for attention." She crosses her arms and sighs, looking around the yard until I notice her eyes land on a tall girl with light russet skin. Her light brown hair is a little longer than mine but hers is frizzy.
"That's Kala. I heard she's good at drawing."

I nod. "Oh yeah, I've seen her art on the wall outside our class before. She's really good. I haven't said 'hi' to her yet though, I feel kinda bad but she always looks so interested in her sketchbook and I don't wanna bother her."

"Let's go say 'hi.'" Anwen responds and starts walking to the shady rocks where Kala is sitting. I look at her sketchbook, she doesn't seem to notice me.

"I like your art." I say with a smile.

Kala's eyes dart up at me and Anwen who are standing in front of her, "Thanks…"

Anwen speaks up, "We're not like Silvia, don't worry. I heard she trashed your drawing last week."
Kala nods and Anwen continues, "Why didn't you speak up about it?"

Kala tears up, "There was no proof she did it, it was my fault anyways. I shouldn't have left my sketchbook out in the open…" the bell rings, signifying the start of the school day. Kala rushes in our grades' line to enter the school. We both drag our feet behind her, not wanting the school day to start. We climb up the six flights of stairs and eventually make it to our floor. Anwen looks drained already and I feel like I'm gonna throw up. We trudge past Ms. Belkin and Ms Octinera's room and somehow manage to enter our own classroom. I speed walk past Damon who's seated beside Kala and slump down on my desk.

Once I'm seated, I notice Diana moving to her seat. She looks haggard, as if she fought in a war only known to mythological heroes. "Did you guys see the protest on John Street?"

I tilt my head in confusion, "Protest?"

Anwen nods, "Oh right, you live north of here. On John Street the anti peace group has been protesting. They like to protest near schools during the beginning of the year."

"Yep! They've been doing that since the Nightmare's got a new leader almost 10 years ago. My parents told me they're hoping the next Saviour will see them and join their cause." Diana responds thoughtfully.

I give them a look of disbelief, "Seriously? Wouldn't the Saviour be like ten? They're trying to recruit a ten year old? That's so dumb."

They laugh and Diana continues, "My parents have been dropping me off at school since they don't want them to bother me. I mean... I know since the new leader took over, the Nightmares have been more aggressive and a lot of people have died... but is war really the answer? Reverie Academy only has a two percent acceptance rate and a bunch of people don't even graduate... At least here in North

America that is." A bunch of our classmates are late, so is Ms. Carvenon.

Anwen groans, "If war breaks out, there's no guarantee that we'd win. That's what these anti peace groups don't understand. Nightmares all have Void Magic which can only be directly and efficiently countered with Aether Magic. We have less than one-hundred people with Aether Magic, not just Reveries, people in general." Oh, I did NOT know that. I mean I knew we didn't have many Aether Magic users but I didn't know it was that little.

"Only a small number of Aether Magic users can create white holes, although healing people is pretty standard. It's the direct opposite of Void Magic. But not all Aether Magic users can use magic on that scale. Every Nightmare has Void Magic and while the world's total population of Reveries likely outnumber them, can we really take any chances? What if the Nightmares are hiding a trump card or something?" Kaine and Mari enter the class and wave at me, I wave back.

She continues, "Even the most talented Aether Magic user at this moment, Ceridwen Chevalier from Team Tyche, had trouble opening a white hole. She's only managed to do it once though and it was really small according to my dad. Really powerful though."

Diana's eyes widen, "Wait, your family knows Ceridwen?! As in the person who took down the previous leader of the Nightmares?!"

Anwen winces, "Yeah? My dad is on Team Tyche, although I guess it's hard to remember just how many Lupo's there are considering a bunch of us are pretty well known. The Chevalier's are family friends, like the Petrova's. People wanted to elevate her to Saviour Status but she didn't meet the mana count. She only got Aether Magic through a core transplant."

I look up in thought, "Hmmm, wasn't there another member of Team Tyche? Aamina Jin, right? She was the tenth Saviour."

Diana looks at me, "Yeah, you're right. I remember seeing news headlines from before we were born about her. I think she died though."

"Technically she's not confirmed dead, she disappeared. A body was found that looked just like her and even matched her dental records except the body looked too young." Anwen reveals in a spooky voice.

I scrunch my nose, "Anwen, don't be creepy."

She laughs, "You're so easy to scare." Diana pouts and Anwen continues, this time in a serious tone.

"Aamina Jin disappeared over a decade ago and there's still no new Saviour, so either she's alive or a new one has been born and we just don't know who they are. If anything she was probably eaten by a wendigo and the corpse they found was probably a girl who looked like Aamina."

"Wendigos exist?" Diana questions.

I nod, "Yeah, some Reverie's who use summoning magic are able to summon them. I assume some Nightmares can too." I look at the clock, 9:10 am. Why hasn't Ms. Carvenon shown up? I hear footsteps coming from the hallway, I guess that must be her. Although I don't hear her heels. Silvia walks in and Diana waves to her. She walks past Damon and Kala before sitting behind me at her desk. I turn my body to face her. Her finger is in a bandage. Is she really trying to fake an injury?

"Is there a problem, Emilia?" Silvia asserts sarcastically.

"No, I was just wondering if you were ok. You haven't been to school since you hurt your finger on Wednesday." I respond as genuinely as I can.

"DAMON hurt my finger, NOT me. He's lucky my mom didn't ask his family to pay for my medical bills." She snarls

I tilt my head in confusion, "We're in Canada... We don't pay for healthcare."

Silvia rolls her eyes and mutters under her breath, "Damn know-it-all." I sigh and turn back to face the board not wanting to deal with this today. I can almost feel Silvia giving me the middle finger from behind my back.

I look back at the clock, it's 9:25 am. Literally half the class isn't here yet. School should've started twenty-five minutes ago, what's going on? This unusual limbo is definitely weird, almost nostalgic. Kinda reminds me of two years ago, being in the hospital room and not knowing what's gonna happen. Except back then I was dying... I look over at the familiar shadow near Anwen in the corner, always following me. I glare at her, the shadow that is. The freaking thing won't leave me alone. All because I wanted to live.

The printer said I'm the Saviour but the Aether Magic I'm supposed to be able to use is slipping through my fingers like sand. The price for my existence... I remember our deal. I probably should've asked for all the terms before agreeing to it though. Didn't think I'd end up gaining Void Magic from it. I thought back to Mr. Atticus's assistant and how she tried to kill me, the shadowy woman must be right. From what I heard, the printer reacts to Aether Magic. That means it must've picked up on what little Aether mana I produce. If I'm producing less, does that mean I'm losing my Saviour status? I look at my hand, creating dark wisps. Yeah, that felt different. Aether Magic has been getting harder and harder to use but what I thought was 'shadow' magic has gotten easier since I started being able to use it two years ago. I didn't think choosing to live would come back to bite me in the butt, but I guess I should read the terms of the deal next time I take one. Not much I can do about it now.

I turn my head to see Lila and Max come into the class and take their seats behind Alice and Catarina's desks. I continue to look around only to make eye contact with Damon. He's not scowling for once, he's just staring at me with wide eyes. I stick my tongue out at him and he scoffs, turning back to his book. I sigh and turn my head to look at Anwen who's also looking at me.

"Is everything alright?" I ask.

"I didn't know you could use shadow magic." She says in a genuine tone.

Well I can't just say I have Void Magic so I guess I gotta lie, "Oh yeah, I've been practicing. Why?"

She smiles, "No reason, I thought you liked using light magic more. Guess you're a jack of all trades then."

I smile back, not feeling even slightly guilty about lying, "You're pretty jack of all trades yourself, you know? You're a genius!" I start hearing the clack of heels coming from the hallway. I check the clock and it's 9:40 am, why is she only coming in now? Marion, Aaron, Alice, Catarina, Cameron and Louis still aren't here.

Ms. Carvenon comes into the class and her eyes start scanning the room. "I'll make an exception for the six of your tardy classmates since it's the first late start of the year but I make no such promises next time." Oh, it's a late start today. Are you kidding me?! I could've slept in! I slump on my desk and groan, Anwen looks away and tries not to snicker at me. October is getting off to a great start.

Chapter 14

"Today Mr. Reynard will be coming back to our class to teach you all how to control your mana because quite frankly, many of you are lacking in that area." I look around and notice my classmates' jaws nearly drop at Ms. Carvenon's blunt explanation of today's events. I raise my hand and Silvia scoffs from behind me.

"Yes, Miss Jang?" Our teacher responds.

I bring my hand down before asking my question, "There's sixteen of us and Mr. Reynard is just one person. Are we doing more partner work or are we being put in groups?"

"Over the course of the afternoon, all of you will get a chance to learn from him one on one here in the classroom while the rest of you do your homework from the morning while you wait for your turn. In my honest opinion, most of you need the one on one time." She answers stoically and without anger. Her voice level and unwavering. I hear coughing and wheezing coming from behind me. I, along with my other classmates, turn to see what's happening only to see Kaine choking on her water. Kaine is definitely trying not to laugh at Ms. Carvenon's insults but our wonderful teacher doesn't need to know that.

She continues, "Any more questions?" Most of us shake our

heads 'no' but Max slowly starts to raise his hand.

"No questions? Good." Max's hand darts back down. The sound of footsteps can be heard from the hallway, they're heavier than any we can make but not angry. It's probably Mr. Reynard.

He enters the class with an air of sadness surrounding him. Is he ever not sad? "Hello, children. I apologize for my tardiness, I had to drop my daughter off at her grandfather's house." Right, he has a daughter named Aaliyah if I remember correctly. I look at Anwen who's beside me and she looks bored out of her mind.

"I'll be calling each of you up, one by one into the hallway." He takes out a toy revolver from his left pocket and holds it up. How I wish my pockets were able to carry, well, anything.

"You'll embed the rubber bullets with mana then shoot me. Typically kids your age aren't able to embed mana into objects very easily but it is a helpful skill regardless of whether you become a Reverie or not." The jaws of my classmates go slack and our eyes widen. Are we seriously going to shoot the guest teacher?

He chuckles and his lips curl up into a soft smile, "Embedding mana into an object is like blowing glass, you need to do it a certain way or it'll break. It could also potentially melt or disintegrate depending on how you do it although the chances of that are only forty percent."

Anwen slides a piece of paper on my desk that reads, "What're the odds Silvia is going to try to shoot us with molten rubber?" I look at her and shrug

Ms. Carvenon speaks up, "I'll be calling you kids in alphabetical order using your first names, in the meantime you all can do the work your teacher assigned you." My eyes canvass class, Mari looks like she's trying to convince Kaine to do the homework but she's slumped over her desk. I can't hear what they're saying but based on how Mari's lips are moving it seems like she's telling Kaine -who stopped slumping- to stop slouching.

"First up, Aaron." Oh great. Aaron's mouth forms a cocky smile as he gets up from his desk behind Damon and walks towards Mr. Reynard. They walk out of the class and we all sit in silence, eager to know what's gonna happen.

"I see you children don't have enough homework to do since you're all sitting and looking at the door." Ms. Carvenon states bluntly, not even looking up from the papers on her desk. While my classmates mostly clamour to get their math books out, I pull out my social studies book.

~~~~~

Time passes and surprisingly, Aaron didn't shoot anyone but the teacher, which is good I guess. The next person to be called is Alice, then Anwen, Cameron, Catarina and Damon. Once Damon is called I
~~~~~

can see Mr. Reynard smile at him.

I can't quite hear what he's saying but it looks like he's asking Damon how his sister is doing. For some reason this really shocks him. I mean, Damon looks really taken aback by this. I wonder why he'd be so surprised about Mr. Reynard asking about Adeline and Yvonne. Maybe he hasn't met his sisters yet? After all, Adeline is an Academy student and I think a year younger than Anastasia. It makes sense that he might not have met her yet. As far as I know though, Yvonne isn't even in school yet so she'd be at home. So wouldnt he have met her? Damon and Mr. Reynard leave the class and enter the hallway.

I turn to Anwen, "Damon looked shocked when Mr. Reynard asked about his sister."

Anwen looks at me with furrowed brows, "That's odd, there was a Thanksgiving charity event on Saturday hosted by the Chevalier's. All the Petrova's went. Me and Anastasia spent most of our time there talking with Adeline and Severus. While Aria was busy playing with Yvonne."

"Don't you guys think Marion doesn't belong here?" Oh great... Silvia.

Silvia continues with a cocky smile, "She's such a weakling, I bet she wouldn't even survive my dad's army training."

Anwen sighs and I put on a smile before saying in my most cheerful voice, "Wow Silvia! I didn't know you did army training!" Silvia scowls at me while Anwen looks back at her math book, trying not to smile. Damon comes back into the classroom.

Anwen -not even looking up from her work- says, "That was quick." I nod back at her.

"Diana? You're up." Ms. Carvenon's voice fills the classroom, it's loud but not angry. Diana gets up and brushes off eraser dust from her dress. Walking up to Mr. Reynard and then into the hall.

~~~~~

Five minutes later, Diana comes back. She looks a little shaken up. I guess the gun looks and feels pretty real then.

Ms. Carvenon calls for me, "Emilia, your turn." I get up from my seat and walk over to Mr. Reynard. I blow my bangs out of my eyes. He's tall, really tall. I stare up at him, he stares down at me and smiles softly. Looking sad as always.

He leads me just outside the classroom to the hallway, we're right outside in between Ms. Octinera's class and Ms Codo's class. He walks over to me, handing over six rubber bullets in one hand and the revolver that shoots them in the other. As the revolver enters my grip my hand drops. It's heavy, way heavier than I thought it'd be.
~~~~~

I start rambling, "So I just embed these with my mana and then I pop these into the gun and shoot you? Or do I pop them in first and then embed them? Or should I embed the whole gun?"

He laughs a little and speaks in a kind tone, "Embed the bullets then put them into the revolver." I have great mana control so I should be good at this. I put the bullets in the pocket of my fanny pack and the gun in my left hand. I take out one of the bullets and force my mana into it. It disintegrates instantly.

"Try using less mana."

"Alright." I respond and take out another bullet. Second time's the charm. I start pouring magic into the bullet. This time it blows up and makes a loud popping sound. I flinch as it pops and the rubber flies everywhere. I'm out of breath and panting. Using magic definitely does drain me despite me being good at it... well, sorta good at it. I've never embedded mana into anything but I'll definitely get it on the third try.

Mr. Reynard smiles as I take out the third bullet. "Use less force and I'm sure you'll get it." Why did he say that?! Now if I don't get it I'll look like a fool! Arghhhhh! Ok ok I got this. I start pouring my mana into the rubber bullet. It's getting hotter, is it supposed to be getting hot? The bullet looks too damaged to put in the gun. I laugh awkwardly and he walks over to me and holds his hand out. I place the damaged bullet in his hands. I try again two more times and I'm unable to properly embed mana into the bullets.

I grab the last bullet in my hand and just put it in the gun, "Can I just shoot you and have that count as partial credit?" I groan.

His mouth curves up in a gentle smile, "You still have one more chance, you know. Statistically most students should be able to get it done by the last try."

I scrunch my nose up. "So...am I not allowed to just shoot you for partial credit?"

He laughs, "Sure, you ca-" I bring up the gun, extending my arms and levelling the gun to my shoulders. Since this belongs to a former Reverie and it's not a foam bullet gun, it likely uses a mana powered "battery" to "power" it rather than gunpowder. I breathe out and pull the trigger. I can feel the recoil going through me. It darts back and I hit myself in the nose. Ow, I was definitely right about it being mana powered though. Foreign mana coursing through me. The bullet hits Mr. Reynard right in the chest.

"As promised, you get partial credit. I'm surprised you managed to hit me since many Canadians have never even seen a real gun in person before, especially at your age."

"I do archery sometimes." I reply while rubbing my nose.

He looks up thoughtfully then says, "Actually, it takes a different 'skill set' to aim and fire a gun accurately than it does to fire an arrow. Although some people are able to master both with comparable outcomes." I stare at him with wide eyes.

"Your form was also off but it was a solid attempt considering this is your first time."

I wasn't expecting him to start rambling like that. It kinda reminds me of Cate though. Now that I think of it, they do have the same eye and hair colour, they both have freckles. Maybe they're related. I heard Kala and Louis are cousins who share the same great grandma. Maybe it's something like that and Cate's family just has really strong genes. Wait no, Cate is adopted. Maybe Mr. Reynard is part of Cate's biological family? You don't see royal blue eyes every day after all. Other than the hair, eyes and freckles though, they look nothing alike. Mr. Reynard looks at me and gestures in the direction of my classroom. I walk past him and into the class. Catarina gives me a thumbs up and tilts her head. I respond with a middle thumb and walk past her to my desk.

I sit down at my desk and Anwen asks, "How was it?"

I groan and slump down on my desk, "I couldn't even embed one bullet. I just shot him square in the chest for partial credit." Kaine gets called up and into the hallway

A voice from behind me starts talking, "I thought you told me you were good at magic, Emilia." Oh great, Silvia.

I turn to look at Silvia, "Look who's talking."

I turn to Anwen, she continues, "How's learning fire magic coming along?"

Diana, who I don't think understands what Anwen is getting at turns to face Silvia and adds, "Oh right! You're learning fire magic from Kaine right?"

Silvia slams her hands on her desk and gets up, walking to the back of the class where Kaine and Mari sit, "Switch with me." She tells Mari.

Mari looks at Silvia with a puzzled expression, "Huh? Why?"

"Now." Silvia commands. Mari grabs her stuff and walks over to Silvia's desk, behind mine. Silvia sits at Mari's desk beside Kaine.

I smile at Mari, "Mari!"

"Mimi!" She responds. We both laugh.

"So, you didn't wanna fight with Silvia today, huh?" Anwen says while doing her homework.

Diana furrows her eyebrows, "You guys were fighting?"

Mari nods, "Yep, I know if I ever had to fight her I'd win but it's not like I wanna start brawling in class." She sighs.

"Do you girls need more work?" We turn to our teacher and vigorously shake our heads, returning back to work.

~~~~~

It's 3:20 pm now, Silvia just walked into the classroom with Mr. Reynard. She looks upset, I guess it didn't go very well. Mr. Reynard goes over to Ms. Carvenon and they start whispering. That's suspicious.

I feel a tap on my back and Mari starts speaking, "Whatcha think they're whispering about, Mimi?"

I turn to face her, "Not sure, but if I had to guess someone's in trouble."
~~~~~

Ms. Carvenon turns to face the class, "Alright children, you all are dismissed." I perk up and start putting my things away.

"Cameron, stay inside for a bit. I need to talk to you." Bingo. I was right.

Aaron starts yelling, "OHHHHH SOMEONES I-"

"Finish that sentence and you'll be staying behind after class too." Ms. Carvenon sighs. She sounds exhausted. Whatever happened must be bad. "Alright class, please thank Mr. Reynard for coming here to help you all today so he can be on his way."

A chorus of "thank you's" echoes through the classroom before smiling and waving to us. I continue putting my books and pencils away as he leaves. It was nice to see he's not as sorrowful as before. I wonder what happened for him to be constantly sad like that... oh well, it's none of my business.

Chapter 15

"Do you think aliens are real?" I wonder out loud. Feeling the cool October air on my skin and getting off the crusty park bench, onto the grass. The stupid looking frog rocker in the distance, staring at me. It knows my secrets.

Cate looks at me and grins, continuing to make a flower crown out of the dandelions he brought from his home, "I'm glad you asked, it is statistically improbable for aliens to not exist." I look at him with curiosity, feeling the grass between my fingers.

"In the event that I roll a die three times in a row and get the numbers one, two, and three, and I then roll the die three times more. I will receive any number of combinations if I keep doing that. Eventually I will roll the same sequence to the first or very similar ones if I keep rolling forever." I smile back at him and his eyes light up with joy and wonder as he talks.

Somehow his fingers are still intricately looping the stems of the dandelions together despite him not looking down to see what he's doing, "Even if aliens are probably not as they are portrayed in movies, the probability of them existing is extremely high."

"That makes sense, so if you keep rolling a die forever, you're bound to get similar results to the first roll eventually. Those results could be looked at as characteristics like intelligence." I look up and respond.

He nods and finishes his flower crown, "Do you think my mom will like it?"

"Of course she will! It's so pretty! I wish I could make flower crowns like that!" I enthusiastically reply. He beams at me and his hair lets off a soft glow. Not very noticeable with the sun out but since I've known him for so long, I can see it just fine.

"I would embed some mana into it to make it glow but I learned last week that I'm really bad at embedding mana into, well, anything." I laugh awkwardly.

He smiles and shakes his head, joining me on the grass, "It's a gift for my mom, you don't need to use your mana for my sake. I know using magic tires you out no matter how talented you are."

"Aw, you think I'm talented?" I grin at him.

He looks at me with wide eyes, "You're super talented! So what if you're not good at embedding mana into objects? Other than that your mana control far exceeds mine."

I move to respond but Cate continues, "Your natural talent is definitely something to be envious of... I wish I had that level of skill. Maybe then my parents wouldn't be afraid of touching my hair."

A cool gust of wind comes through, messing up both our hairstyles, "You're the only one who has faith that my hair won't sting you. I know my parents tried and probably got conditioned into not touching my hair without gloves, but it still hurts that they don't trust me not to sting them anymore."

He looks down at his dandelion flower crown and I place my hand on his shoulder, "You didn't sting people on purpose. It's only natural you wouldn't know how to control your Specialty Magic since you had no one to teach you."

He pouts, "Then how come you don't have any problems with it?"

I laugh, "I'm just that good, I guess. It might have to do with the fact that I never worried about hurting anyone. Maybe it's 'cause Oppa was there to teach me magic. Either way,"
I lift my hand and create dim little bursts of light around us, "I just had confidence in myself. I think that you've come a long way and that one day you'll be one of the strongest Reverie's around."

His eyes light up, "You really think so?"

I nod, "I know s-"

"Oh look, it's the Showy Susie." I turn to look behind me, great, just great. What is Damon doing here?

He sits down beside Cate on the grass and starts talking in a low voice, "You both should really be more aware of your surroundings." Me and Cate look at each other in confusion.

"In the distance, there's someone watching you."

Cate and I tense up and Damon sighs, "I'll remain here with you both for now but you should really think about getting somewhere safe."

I look at him, confused, "Why exactly are you helping us? I mean, you could've let the stalker or whatever over there kidnap us or something."

He responds, "Because the rest of our peers are frankly, dull and unassuming. While you are also weak and quite evidently disabled, the amount of mana you have makes you the closest of our peers to be equal to me. That's all it is." My jaw drops slightly and I make eye contact with him. Nope that's gross, I hate eye contact. Also, WHAT THE HECK?! Obviously I know I'm disabled but he didn't have to point it out like that! Literally the most backhanded compliment ever. I look at Cate then Damon, then Cate again, then down on the ground. Cate pulls out a few strands of his hair, turning each individual strand into a different jellyfish. He's not able to use any actually deadly ones yet but he's probably thinking this should deter the stalker over by the trees.

Damon looks up at the handful of jellyfish surrounding us, "Smart, despite these particular ones being harmless creatures, most wouldn't even be able to tell the difference between the harmless and the ones that make you go insane from the pain."

My eyes widen and I respond using a genuine tone, "Wow, I never knew you could be nice."

"Millie! That's mean!" Cate chastises me.

Damon scoffs and gets up from the grass, urging us up too, "I'm not 'nice' I'm honest. I'm able to praise others when it is deserved. Now, my place isn't far from here so you both can either join me and get away from potential danger or you can stay here and possibly get hurt." Me and Cate jolt up and follow Damon. The jellyfish following us

"Aye aye, Captain!" We both respond and Damon scowls. He begins walking down the path behind the crusty dusty bench. We walk past the little shed. Why's there a shed at the park? Who knows but we walk past it and start heading down the ravine via the boardwalk. We're surrounded by trees and dirt, although it's definitely sketchy considering the circumstances, it's probably safer than passing by the stalker and going the long way to what I assume is Damon's house. Me and Cate look at each other, then at Damon who's walking in front of us

I turn to Cate and whisper urgently, "Wait, what if he's trying to kidnap us?"

He sighs, "The chances of me falling for a ruse like that are extremely low."

I look at him and tilt my head, "What about me?"

He smiles gently, "I'm surprised you haven't gotten kidnapped by now."

"I'm not that stupid!" I yell as we continue walking.

Damon stops in his tracks and turns to face us, "Shut up! I don't understand why anyone would even want to take you ingrates!"
He sighs and moves his hair out of his face, "The next moment either of you mentions anything about me kidnapping you, I will leave you here to get abducted by your pursuer." He continues walking. Me and Cate look at each other and shrug, following him. We pass some dirt and trees and rocks and trees and dirt and rocks and trees, basically just a lot of brown, grey and green. We get to some stairs and start climbing down it. As we walk down the stairs I come to the realization that neither me or Cate have told our moms where we're going...

I try to speak up, "Um... Damon?"

"What?" He responds bluntly.

I look at Cate then at Damon as we continue walking down onto the brick road, "We uh... didn't tell our moms we were going to your place."

Cate looks back at me and nods sheepishly, "Yeah... thanks for saving us bu-"

He cuts Cate off, "You may contact your mothers once we reach my abode." Cate stares at me but continues to follow after Damon. We walk past some modern houses and by another park, this one with a river running through. At least I think it's a river.
"At least she didn't attempt to fire projectiles at others." Damon mutters

I tilt my head in confusion "Huh?"

Damon sighs, "The reason that pest for a classmate got dropped from the class was because he had attempted to fire the revolver on another educator's classroom." My eyes widen. So that's why Cameron got dropped.
"I'm simply stating that you are far more tolerable than he was."

I force a smile, "Thanks...? I guess?" He doesn't stop walking and merely nods in response. We continue passing more houses, though this time the houses are more a more classic design. The typical red brick type of house if you will.

"Wait, if we're being stalked then is it really a good idea to lead the stalker to your house?" We turn a corner and Damon walks up the walkway to a large house before grabbing his keys and unlocking the door.

Damon rolls his eyes, "Do you really believe a stalker will attempt to injure a Petrova?" Ya' know what? That's fair enough. Me and Cate walk into the surprisingly modern home . It may look like an older home from the outside but the inside definitely looks new. I guess they've been doing renovations or something. Damon follows after us and closes the door, the click of the lock sending shivers down my spine. I look at Cate who's looking at me, his breathing uneven. I think he realized we just walked into the house of a stranger. Damon takes his shoes off in the entrance and walks in.

I hear a woman's voice echo the house, she sounds kind, "Damon? Is that you?"

Damon sighs, "Yes, mother. I am being accompanied by a fellow classmate and a potential associate." I look around the house and take my shoes off, Cate follows suit. The layout of the house is pretty similar to the Lupo's from what I can see. It's just much bigger, obviously. I mean, considering eight people live here, I think the house is a good size for the family. Footsteps echo the house from the upper floor until a woman with mixed blonde and lavender hair appears at the top of the stairs. She's holding a toddler in her arms. That must be Yvonne.

The woman smiles gently at us, "I'm so glad you've made friends, Damon." She starts walking down the stairs with little Yvonne in her arms,

"My name is Azalea Desiderio Petrova, what are your names?"

Cate hesitantly responds, "My name is Cato Evermore."

He nudges me with his elbow, "My name is Emilia Jang, I'm Damon's classmate. It's nice to meet you."

Cate continues, "Sorry for the intrusion, Damon offered to bring us here since we were at Lisa Park and someone had been following us."

Mrs. Petrova's eyes narrow at us, "I'll bring this up with my husband and alert the police."

She sits down on the bottom steps and places Yvonne in her lap, "If someone is trying to prey on children, it is important that we adults keep you kids safe. Please don't leave the house until a parent or guardian comes to get you both." We nod and I tell Mrs. Petrova my mom's phone number. She calls my mom and explains the situation, telling her I'm safe and that Cate is with me.

She hangs up and gives us a reassuring smile, "Alright, Emilia. Your mom said that your dad would pick you both up in half an hour."

I stiffen up but force a smile, "Thank you so much!"

Chapter 16

As I climb the last of the six flights of stairs my lungs start screaming for air "I hate my life." I groan.

Anwen's laboured breathing beside me tells me that she too hates her life, she groans, "Kill me now." Called it.
A look of realization crosses her face, "Oh...no..."

Huh? That's not good, please let the answer of my question be only mildly bad, "'Oh no'? What do you mean 'Oh no'?"

Anwen grimaces, "We were supposed to meet the class in the gym today... I forgot 'cause we usually skip lunch recess if we have a guest here..."

My eyes widen and my jaw slackens. You've got to be kidding, "So we climbed up SIX flights of stairs... FOR NOTHING?!" She nods and we both let out dissatisfied groans

"Come on, let's go to the gym. Ms. Carvenon will be mad that we're late." She starts walking ahead of me, dragging her feet as her breathing starts to even out. I follow suit.

"The guest is a student from the Academy, right?" I ask as I follow Anwen past Ms. Octinera's, Ms. Belkin and Ms. Codo's class towards the first flight of stairs.

She nods in response, "Yeah, his name is Ivory and he's in the same class as Anastasia. He's been to my house before." We walk past Ms. Akt's class and towards the next set of stairs.

As we descend, I ask, "He must be really strong if he got chosen to represent the academy."

We continue down the last stretch of stairs before Anwen continues, "He is, regardless of what other people say, he's really talented." I tilt my head in confusion and she stops at the bottom of the stairs to look at me.

"Some people dislike the fact that a black kid from an unknown family is able to go toe to toe with Anastasia, the pride of the Lupo's."

Anwen crosses her arms and leans on the wall, "I just don't get it. Reveries are the profession with the highest mortality rate, what difference does the colour of someone's corpse make if they're dead. At the end of the day, we all bleed red."

I can tell Anwen is really upset about this. It's only natural after all, to be upset at the unfair treatment of others, "I guess their 'no bullying' policy isn't held up very well."

Anwen laughs, "No kidding. Ivory has to hold himself back and let Anastasia win so he doesn't get harassed. It's awful."

"Wait, we should probably get to the gym." I respond frantically.

Anwen's eyes widen, "I completely forgot about that, let's run so it doesn't look like we took our time." I nod and we book it past the doors and into the gym.

The stern voice of our teacher echoes the gym as we enter, panting and heaving, "I see you girls took your time getting here." Frick. The entire class looks at us. I make eye contact with Damon and he sticks his tongue out at me. That little brat. There's an older boy standing beside Ms. Carvenon, his onyx black hair, lavender irises and eye shape makes him look a little like me. The only thing that would set us apart is his deep ochre skin.

The boy, who I assume is Ivory, has a calm and kind demeanour. He turns to Ms. Carvenon and says, "Before you get too angry, you should determine the reason for them being late and if it's valid then we should cut them some slack."

Our teacher sighs, "Very well."

She turns to me and Anwen, "So what exactly could be the cause for your tardiness? The gym is on the first floor."

We tense up and I confidently say, "Sorry Miss, I forgot my inhaler in class and Anwen came with me to go get it."

"Alright then, take a seat on the floor with your classmates." She responds and turns to face the rest of the class as we rush to sit down.

"As you know, today we have a special guest from the Academy." She looks at Ivory, "Feel free to introduce yourself."

He takes a step towards us, "Hello class, my name is Ivory Ishiodori and I'm a student representative of Reverie Academy. Even though the acceptance rate is only two percent, if you do manage to get in, the curricular activities and programs are easy to get invested in. They will help you become a strong and competent Reverie as well as learn more about yourself." We all look at Ivory in awe. A real Academy student is here in the room with us and according to Anwen, he's super strong!

"The test you will be receiving today is beating me in a trial of combat." We're screwed. "Any volunteers?"

Mari raises her hand, "I'll go."

"The rest of you, move to sit on the stage." Ms. Carvenon says while leading us towards the side stairs of the stage. Ivory puts his fist out and one by one we start fist bumping him as we walk up on the stage. His face beaming with excitement. He must be really happy to be here. I move to fist bump him. His fist tightens slightly. Did he just tense up? He grins at me. Maybe I imagined it, so why does he look kinda uneasy? I get up on the stage and see Damon shake his hand. Ivory's eyes widen and his body tenses. I guess he got a closer look at him and realized that Damon's a Petrova.

Damon glares at Ivory, which to be fair he glares at everyone, "Is there something wrong?"

Ivory grins and says, "No nothing is wrong, thanks for participating."

He turns to Mari and holds his hand out, his smile kind and reassuring, "I'm glad you're willing to fight. Oh and feel free to use magic." They both make eye contact with each other and Mari grins wider than I've ever seen her grin before. Ivory crouches down and places his palm on the ground, the floor and walls start glowing lavender.

"I enforced the walls and floor with a basic protection spell, feel free to go all out." He gets back up, the kind smile never leaving his face.

"First one on the floor loses."

Marin has a smug look on her face, her chin raised, "Of course." To be fair, if I had her Specialty Magic I'd be cocky too.

"Are you both ready?" Ms. Carvenon asks from the back of the stage. Mari and Ivory give a thumbs up and she starts counting down from ten.

Ivory steps closer to Mari and smiles gently at her, "Goodluck."

My classmates join our teacher in counting down, "Three, Two, One." Mari gets on her toes and starts spinning before Ivory rushes at her. Mari, what're you doing? Stop spinning! He lifts his knee up and pivots. I've seen this before... he snaps kicks, hitting her in the stomach. She falls to the ground, landing on her butt. Mari's eyes are wide open, she's trembling. Ivory brings his leg back in and places his foot back on the floor. Was that Taekwondo? The class is silent as Mari looks up at Ivory. What just happened?

Anwen says from beside me, "That's his Specialty Magic."

I look at her with confusion, "That's the reason he shook Marin's hand and gave us all fist bumps."

"That was a good shot, you almost had me there." Ivory smiles and helps Mari up. She looks shaken up but she heads up to the stage and sits beside me.

"Would anyone else like to give it a try?"

Silvia raises her hand, "Me." Ivory beckons her over and Silvia jumps down the stage, walking over to him.

Mari, still trembling, clings onto my arm, "He used my own magic against me."

She whispers. Her grip gets tighter, "Is that what it feels like to have your freedom stripped away...?"

Her voice starts shaking, "I get it now, I understand why everyone was so upset when I used my magic on them in kindergarten." Right, back then when she just started being able to use magic, she used to control our classmates as a prank. Adults used to praise her for her confidence until they learned the only reason she would make eye contact with others was so she could 'prank' them.

I place my hand on hers and lightly squeeze, "You're safe, Mari. It's okay now." Our classmates start counting down from ten.

She buries her face in my arm as she speaks in a low voice, "Is that why everyone's parents said our classmates couldn't be friends with me before...? I'm really sorry. I didn't mean to make them into a puppet. I just thought it was funny. I didn't know it was so scary. Were you scared when I did it to you?" Silvia holds her fists up like a boxer, although her form seems off. Her elbows are too far out.

I look back at Mari, "It's ok, Mari. I used my threads to make you a puppet too, remember? We're even. Both our parents got so mad when I used my threads so you could swing from the tree in Jacob's yard." I smile at her and she nods.

"You were excited about getting lucky enough to have Specialty Magic. Most of the kids in our class were already able to use magic." I take out a tissue from my fanny pack and hand it to her.

The match starts, "Yeah it was wrong but you didn't do it again as a prank since the end of senior kindergarten. The times after you did do it, you were defending others." That's good, she's not trembling as bad anymore.

"Wanna watch Silvia fight?" She nods and we look towards Ivory who already closed the gap despite Silvia rapidly backing up. Ivory grabs forearm and yanks it down, he's obviously not using much force but being bigger and stronger than Silvia definitely isn't helping. Once she's almost on the floor Ivory sweeps her feet causing Silvia to fall on the ground.

"That was good but your elbows were too far out and you would've had a better shot if you tried to put distance between us using magic." Ivory smiles and extends her arm to help her up. Silvia rolls her eyes and gets up on her own. She definitely didn't appreciate being told her form was wrong and that she should've used magic. After all, once the topic of combat comes up, she doesn't shut up about it. She's also awful at magic although that part isn't her fault.

Silvia trudges back on the stage.

"I shall go next." Damon states from behind me. He jumps off the stage and looks at Ivory.

"Start the countdown." We all look at each other and awkwardly start counting down from ten. Ivory looks a little nervous, his body stiffens up as he gets into a ready position. Whether he's worried about the fact that Damon's a pompous rich kid or the fact that he's basically superhuman, I don't know. What I do know is that he should be more scared.

"Three, Two, One!" Lavender threads attach to Damon's arm. Wait, that's MY Specialty Magic! Ivory yanks the threads down while Damon grabs the threads and pulls. Ivory almost loses his footing, he definitely wasn't expecting that. I stare at them in disbelief. Obviously I know he can use other people's magic, Mari literally just told me. The reality of the situation just sank in now I guess. Damon pulls again before darting towards Ivory who lets the threads disappear. The height deficient one jabs his hand into the other's diaphragm. Ivory hunches over and heaves, leaving an opening for Damon to sweep his feet. Ivory lands on the floor. Well that's upsetting, I was hoping Damon could get an ego check. We're all silent, waiting for one of them to move.

Damon lowers himself to Ivory's level and whispers, "The difference between you and me is that I know what it's like to face death. You've lived in a comfortable environment, not knowing suffering." Which, uh, seems kinda dramatic if you ask me. Maybe I'm wrong though since I lip read that.

Chapter 17

Another day, another duel class. At least it's a duel so we're allowed to use magic.

Ms. Carvenon walks in front of me, "Emilia, you're partnered up with Damon." …WHAT?! My eyes widen and I can almost see my life flashing before my eyes. I'm so so SO screwed. My classmates murmurs echo the gym. The blue walls seemingly getting smaller and smaller as I really take in how UTTERLY screwed I am.

I turn to Damon and smile, "I look forward to dueling with you." He scowls and walks to the center of the gym. Our teacher already having reinforced the walls and floor with magic.

Alice places her hand on my shoulder as our classmates start heading to the left and right so they can get on the stage, "You gonna be ok?"

My expression must've been one of impending doom because she continues, "Remember what Anwen said?"

She gets closer and starts speaking in a low voice, "Damon's not very good at magic, and with your Specialty Magic, you just need to stop him before he reaches you."

I smile, "Thank you." She smiles back reassuringly before heading to the stage. I move to the centre of the court. I look down at the floor, the markings of literally every sport etched onto it.

I look up at Damon whose bored expression is making me think twice about Alice's strategy, "Do you really believe you can best me? You're a charlatan at best so try not to get any ideas." I stare at him with wide eyes. Ok, I'm going to pummel him. Our classmates start counting down from ten.

"Ten." I stand up straighter.

"Nine." I widen my stance.

"Eight." Why isn't Damon doing anything?

"Seven." We make eye contact.

"Six." I look away.

"Five!" Damon puts one leg in front of the other.

"Four!" Oh frick, he's gonna run at me.

"THREE!" He moves his hair out of his face. This is a duel right?

"TWO." We're not supposed to be getting physical! I'm so screwed.

"ONE." I put my hands up in a ready position. This might as well happen.

"BEGIN!" Damon rushes at me but luckily for me my threads connect to his arms and legs before he gets too far. The amethyst strings being my saviour. I see my friends from the corner of my eye.

Huh? Why does Alice look like she's witnessing a crime? Wait, what's that black thing darting towards me? Is it coming from Damon? Void Magic, that's Void Magic. Why does he have Void Magic? I feel something warm spreading through my left wrist. It's wet. Wet? I dissipate my threads and bring my hands down in front of me. Blood, shouting, more blood. I can't hear anything. Damon is looking at me, he looks... scared? Like he didn't mean to do that, like he lost control for a second. The blood is dripping down my arm and onto the floor. I bring my wrist down and press the bottom of my shirt against the wound. There's a lot of blood. It's soaking through the fabric. My hand is red, my hand is wet, my hand is warm. There's more yelling. Alice is by my side in an instant.

Ms. Carvenon is with Damon, she's pointing at the wall. "Go to the office!" I think she's saying. Alice holds my arm and drags me out of the gym and towards the office. Rushing past the wall of grad photos, we reach the office. The principal looks shocked once she sees us. She gets us some clean towels since I imagine they don't have gauze. The receptionist picks up the phone, she's probably calling my parents.

~~~~~

I don't know how much time passed since I came to the office but eventually my wrist stops bleeding. I must've had a flesh wound or they would've called an ambulance.
~~~~~

I see my mom and dad rush into the school, "Emilia!" I can hear again.

"Mom? Dad?" I look at them. They hug me and start checking me. My dad gently grabs my forearm and slowly takes off the bloody towel. His demeanour changes instantly. He's mad.

"What happened?" He's really mad. I stay silent.

He says again, "Emilia, what happened?" Please don't start yelling, don't yell at me, don't yell at me, please don't yell at me.

Alice pipes up, "We were sparring in class using mana and her opponent freaked out and used magic to cut her."

My dad turns to Alice, "Thank you, it seems like Emilia is still shaken up by it." He's angry. I know he's not angry at me. So why do I feel the need to run and hide?

He turns to the office staff and thanks them before turning to my mom, "Take her to the car, she'll feel better in a more comfortable environment." My mom nods and brushes my hair behind my ear. She holds my right hand as we walk out of the office.

"I have gauze and iodine in the car. We'll clean the wound and patch you up good as new." My mom smiles at me, I smile back. We follow my dad in the direction of the gym. I guess they parked by the north yard. We walk past the graduate photos on the wall and climb the few steps till we see the gym. Mr. Petrova comes rushing in the north doors with Mrs. Petrova and Yvonne. He sees us and places a hand on his wife's shoulder. He says something to her. He rushes into the gym while Mrs. Petrova walks towards us.

She looks solemn, "Hello, I'm Azalea Desiderio Petrova, Matthew's wife. I'm also Damon's stepmother."

My mom looks confused but responds, "I'm Alma Velasquez."

Mrs. Petrova opens her mouth to continue but gets interrupted by my dad yelling from the gym, "YOUR SON IS A NIGHTMARE?!" I tense up. The gym bursts into commotion and everyone starts yelling. Damon is a Nightmare? I know he has Void Magic because I felt it when he cut me, but still. My mom apologizes to Mrs. Petrova and rushes me past the gym, into the north yard and to the car. She opens the door and gets into the back seat with me, grabbing a box with supplies from the front seat.

She opens the bottle of iodine and a gauze packet, putting the iodine on the gauze. "Tell me if it hurts." She says before lightly dabbing the cut with the gauze.

I wince, "It's cold." She smiles and continues. Once she finishes, she gets another gauze packet and opens it. She folds it and places it on my wrist and starts putting tape on it.

She places the last piece of tape on it, "There, good as new." Her expression gentle and warm.

My eyes feel heavy, "You must be tired."

She brings me in to rest my head on her lap, "Try to sleep for a bit." I close my eyes and release the tension in my body.

<div align="center">~~~~~</div>

A dark room. No, not a room... the void. Why am I back here? I look around at the endless sea of nothing. Not black, nothing. Well, I guess it's more like dark nothing. I bring my left wrist up, no bandage, no cut. Actually, my hands are small, too small.

"Hello, Emilia Jang." Her voice calls out from behind me.

I turn around to face her, "Who are you? Where am I?" Oh... this dream again. I guess it's more like a memory than a dream.

"You're dying." Right, she never did answer my second question. I had to figure out this was the void myself.

I say the same thing I did back then, "I know." It's not like I'm able to say anything else.

"You don't want to live?" She comes closer to me. I'm unable to make out any of her features. All I know is that she's a woman, a very beautiful and very vengeful woman.

"Are you a demon or something?"

She looks shocked but I continue, "You're here to take something from me so I can live, right?"

She laughs, "Demon? Well, it's not the first time I've been associated with him."

I open my mouth to speak but she interrupts me, rude, "However you're correct to assume I'm offering you a way to cheat death."

I respond, though not of my own will, "Don't lie, there's no cure for cancer. At least not when you're this close to death…" My eight year old self seems very logical. Already knowing how utterly screwed she is. Already knowing the chances of living to adulthood were slim.

"Let's just say I do have a way." She places her right palm on my left shoulder.

I roll my eyes and shrug off her hand, "You gonna ask for my soul or something?"

She smiles wide, "No, I don't want your soul. I only want one thing."

"What are you gonna take?" I respond. Back then I was thinking about my mom. How she'd be sad if I died.

"I won't take anything, rather, I'll give you something."

"Which is?" I question. The void is dark, yet not dark. There's no light, yet I can see.

"You'll see." I stare at her dumbfounded, this is so sketchy.

She continues, "What's the fun in telling you?"

"Huh?" Internally I laugh, younger me was so confused.

She smiles, "All you need to know is that it'll help you complete the task I'm giving."

I try to talk but again, she interrupts me, "As for what that task is, I want you to fight. I want you to struggle and claw your way to victory. Destroy everything in your path if you have to."

I still don't know what her goal is but since the deal wasn't bad, I accepted, "That sounds easy enough. I'll do it."

Her face contorts into a sinister grin. Probably not a great sign, "What's your name again?"

She presses her index finger to my forehead, "Call me, A."

~~~~~

I'm being rolled into an MRI machine. My body feels weak. I remember being upset, or rather, feeling numb but acting cranky due to all the medication that the deal wasn't fulfilled. Ten minutes pass by, the machine is loud. Twenty minutes pass by, I'm falling asleep to the rhythm of the clanks. Thirty minutes pass by, the sound of hammers in a washing machine is continuing on and on. Forty minutes pass by, then fifty. Finally I'm taken out of the machine. My mom helps me into the wheelchair. We pass the other x-ray rooms and the colourful walls. Wheeling me past the reception and to the elevator. We enter the unit, the walls are colourful, too colourful. We wave to the nurses and head to my room. Room eleven, fitting seeing as I was the eleventh patient in this clinical trial.

I'm not sure how long we waited but eventually my doctor rushes in, "Alma! Alma! It's gone! Your daughter is cancer free!" My mom starts crying. A. really cured me.

She continues frantically, "We're not sure how, we thought the
~~~~~

cancer had come back."

She smiles at us, "Your daughter will live, Alma."

I open my eyes to the car pulling into the driveway, "Did you have a good nap?" My dad asks. I nod and put on a smile, like I always do.

"Good." He responds. I'll fake being human. Even if I'm just a Nightmare, I'll pretend I'm their happy go lucky cancer survivor daughter. All to protect the peace I have now.

Chapter 18

The car pulls up to the north yard, its lunch recess right now. It took a lot of convincing, from me, the school and my brother, but eventually we managed to convince my parents into sending me back to school. Finding out that Damon's a Nightmare had definitely shaken things up. The whole neighbourhood is talking about it, even other schools are talking about it.

I open the car door and say "Bye." to my mom.

She looks unnerved. "You have your hearing aids in your bag, right?"
I give her a thumbs up. "Good, make sure you wear them. Also, remember, you're going home with Anwen today after school."

Nodding my head, "I remember, and I'll try to wear them, no promises though! The world is too loud with them." I say goodbye once again and I start walking down the sidewalk to the south yard.

A., who's following me says, "Why do you pretend?" We pass by the bus stop.

"I don't know who I am if I don't. Besides, I don't want to burden my mom." She passes me and smiles.

"You seem awfully happy." We pass the crosswalk before entering the school.

"Even if I'm a monster, a Nightmare, I want to protect my mom." I turn left and enter the office.

"Oh, Emilia, welcome back." The receptionist smiles warmly at me.

I smile back, "Hello, Ms. Hannah. How are you?"

Her smile is sickeningly sweet, "So polite, you are. I'm good, thank you for asking. You're signing in for the day, right?" I nod and she starts typing before turning to her right and grabbing me a sign in slip.

She hands it to me, "Now off you go. Tell your teacher that I say 'hi'."

"Will do!" I say. The bell rings, signalling the end of recess. Ya know what? I'm not gonna climb those six flights of stairs. I'm gonna take the long way to class. I walk out of the office and turn left instead of going straight. I walk past the grad photo hall and past the washrooms. I climb up the quarter flight of stairs till I see the gym. This may be the long way but there's less stairs this way so obviously it's the better way. I turn right past the sad empty space where a vending machine used to be and I start climbing the two half flights of stairs. I walk past Ms. Akt's room and make another left past the blue doors and up the other stairs. By this point I'm struggling to breathe but I NEED to get to class before my classmates. I finally make it to the top. Sitting down by the door to class in an attempt to catch my breath. I hear the loud click of the doors by the stairs and immediately get up. Still heaving, I try to compose myself so I can brag about how slow they are. The grade four line enters my sight. They turn and walk into Ms. Octinera's class. The other grade five class right behind them, they enter Ms. Belkin's class that's parallel to Ms. Octinera's classroom. My class enters my sight, Ms. Carvenon leading the line.

I step away from the door, "Good afternoon, Ms. Carvenon."

She approaches me and swiftly unlocks the door, "Welcome back, Emilia. I am unsure if you've heard, but we are going to be doing the simulation exam today." My classmates start heading inside the class. Frick, I am so not ready for an exam. Maybe she'll let me do it another day?

"I will explain in more detail once you're all seated. Feel free to take the next five minutes to mentally prepare for it." Yeah, that checks out. This might as well happen. I walk into class, past the whiteboard and to my desk.

Once I sit down, a loud voice comes from one of the desks behind me, "Aaron, you owe me five bucks!" I turn to see Louis standing up.

Aaron, who's sitting behind Damon, groans, "Ugh, fine! I'll give it to you after school."

I guess my expression is one of confusion 'cause Anwen speaks up from beside me, "They were betting on whether you died or not. You suddenly stopped coming to school so they thought you either bled out or got cancer again, idiots. Everyone knows cancer doesn't kill you that fast." I stare at her with my mouth open. Did my classmates really think I died? They didn't even bother to check up on me, rude.

I gather my composure before responding, "Please tell me you didn't think I died."

She looks me dead in the eye before saying, "Of course not, Catarina and Diana are another story though."

I whip my head to the right to look at Catarina who immediately looks down at her hands, "I'm glad you're not dead…?"

"Why was that phrased like a question?" I respond.

The stern voice of our teacher echoing the classroom, "Alright class, now that you've settled in let's begin." I turn to face the teacher who's standing up tall.

"I expect you all know what's happening today?"

I start to raise my hand but she continues, " Today is your simulation exam. Though you've done no actual preparation for it, this will be your time to show me your survival skills." Wait, survival skills? I don't like the sound of that. She holds up these funky looking stickers, they look like the stickers they use for ECG's.

"You will place one on your neck, once that's done you may put your head down on your desk." Sounds straightforward enough.

She walks past the rows of desks and shows us the stickers, "Once everyone is set, I'll use magic to link you all up. You'll be put into a shared dream." Wait, that's actually really cool. What's the downside?

I think Anwen has the same question because she speaks up, "Are there any restrictions in place?" My classmates look dumbfounded -except for Damon of course- they clearly hadn't even thought of that.

Ms. Carvenon smiles, "Good question, Miss Lupo."

She returns to the front of the class, "You'll be stranded in one of the border towns by the Intermedial, there will be Spawned type Nightmares wandering around and you'll be unable to use magic." The atmosphere of the class shifts. Magic is so ingrained in our society that being without it is super scary. I mean, having no mana is considered a disability after all. Kinda like how people with glasses are technically disabled and glasses are the disability aid. As ordinary as it seems, it still affects your daily life.

"All you'll have with you is a quillon dagger and a semiautomatic pistol" Oh great, we're giving Damon and Silvia weapons. Damon wouldn't hurt someone unless provoked so I'm not too worried about that. Silvia though? I really hope I don't bump into her.

Alice raises her hand and Ms. Carvenon nods to signal for her to start speaking, "How are we being graded?"

"You will be stuck in the simulation until the end of the school day. Once the time is up you'll wake up. If you die or get knocked unconscious you will wake up." My eyes widen. Did she just say 'if you die'?

"I will be seeing how long you can remain in the simulation and your mental state once you come out." Oh lovely, this is gonna traumatize us, isn't it. She starts going around the room, handing us each a sticker and one by one we put them on our neck.

She hands me mine, "Thank you." I say. She smiles at me and I fold my arms on my desk and rest my head on them. I close my eyes. I wonder what it's gonna feel like. Oh frick, I forgot to ask how many of our senses we'll be keeping. Oh well.

I'm in a house, well, more like what's left of a house. The roof is fine but the walls of the home are clearly damaged. Like, most of it is missing, kind of damaged. Wait, I don't feel wind on my legs. I look down and notice I'm wearing a black, lightweight, long sleeved jumpsuit . Lucky me, this probably means I'm gonna have to run for my life. At least I'm wearing running shoes I guess. She could've made me wear sandals. There's a gun holster under my armpit, I play with the button. Hopefully I'll be able to use it in a split second if needed... wait, on my left leg there's a pouch, on my right there's the dagger. Please, please, PLEASE tell me the gun is already loaded. Maybe I should find Damon, he'll probably know how to load a gun.
I walk around the rundown house, using my foot to tap the floor ahead of me before stepping. I'm not taking chances with the floor swallowing me up. A loud crack echoes the house. Nope! I'm getting out! I speed-walk out of the house.

Someone grabs my hand and starts dragging me away from the house, "Emilia! Let's go!"

I look at the person I hope to team up with, "Alice?! You have no idea how happy I am-"

"Oh my god, just run!" She exclaims, holding my hand. I do as I'm told. A snarl comes from one of the houses we pass. I look back at the rundown buildings -still running- to see a giant deer-like creature standing on its hind legs, only this creature has the face of a chimpanzee. The hands too... It spots us.

I speed up, "Alice, run faster!"

"We should be able to outrun it at this speed." She's not speeding up, we need to run faster!

"Alice! That's a chimp! Haven't you noticed?! We have all our senses here! If it catches us we're gonna die a painful death! Simulation or not, I don't want to get ripped apart!" I guess she got the memo because her eyes widen and she starts trembling. Man, this is a bad day to have emotions. My fight or flight mode is definitely activated. We run past a bunch more buildings before I drag her into a house. Like all the other houses it's run down but this one has more wall protection. I'm running out of breath, I won't be able to outrun it.

"Is your gun loaded?" I ask.

Alice's eyebrows are furrowed, "Huh, what-"

"Is your gun loaded? We're gonna have to fight that Nightmare and our guns are our best bet." I take my gun out of its holster, I start looking at it. How do I check if it's loaded? There's gotta be a button or switch somewhere. I press a button behind the trigger and the magazine pops out.

Loaded, thank god it's loaded, "Alice, get your gun out. They came loaded. You stay there and I'll go by the door way." I point to the entryway of the barren room.

"Once the Nightmare comes in we'll both shoot it, don't go for a headshot, just try to hit it." She straightens up and nods.
A crash resonates through the house. I think it broke down a wall. I quickly reload the gun and Alice takes her own out. Loud screeches follow. There's a rapid thudding sound. Is it running? That's much faster than its speed when it was chasing us. Was it...toying with us? I grip the gun tightly in both hands. Hopefully I'm holding it right, probably not though. Oh... why did it just occur to me that no one ever really taught us how to shoot a gun? Even when Mr. Reynard visited, he only told me that my form was off but he didn't teach me what proper form looks like. We are so screwed aren't we. Bang! Did Alice just shoot? Wait. My eyes widen and I turn towards Alice, bringing my gun up. Bang! How is it that fast?! I put my finger on the trigger and aim at the Nightmare's head. I don't wanna shoot Alice after all. Bang! My arms feel the force of the recoil. Bang! I'm surprised I didn't hit myself in the nose again since the guns Reverie's use have much more recoil. Bang! Maybe this gun is a normal gun. I wouldn't know. The Nightmare falls on the floor, we managed to hit it in the chest and head.

Chapter 19

I walk up to it and press the barrel of the gun at its head. I gotta make sure it's dead, after all. I shoot it again before walking up to Alice who's sitting on the floor. I give her a reassuring smile to which she mirrors me.

"Don't you think that was a bit overkill?" She wrinkles her nose and I take one hand off the gun, offering it to her.

She takes it and I respond, "I'd rather be sure it's dead than see your face get ripped off."

I pull her up and she shrugs, "Fair enough. I'd rather keep my face on."

Her mouth curves into a snarling frown as she looks behind me, "Oh my- is it melting?!" I turn to look at the Nightmare behind me, lo and behold, it's melting.

I gag, "Oh god, that's disgusting. Is that what that smell was?."

We decide to hurry out of the room. Walking into the main area of the now sufficiently destroyed house.

Once we're away from the goop and the smell, Alice speaks up, "What should we do now? We have no way of knowing how long it's been or how much longer is left."

I look up in thought, "We should probably just try and hide."

I look down at the gun in my hand, "We don't have magic so I doubt there are many if any Nightmares above calibre three. Since we have limited ammo we shouldn't go looking for a fight."

"I agree, I really don't wanna smell Nightmare goo again." She shudders. She takes my hand and we walk around the house, passing the kitchen and dining room. For some reason the entire house seems to be made of spruce wood. We get to the back of the stairs and sit underneath. It's strange, despite the fact that we just used a gun for the first time, this is strangely peaceful.

Maybe it's because A. isn't here, "You look like you have a lot on your mind, want to talk about it?"

I look up, trying to decide whether to answer or not, "What makes a human a human?"

Her eyes widen, "Hmm... if it were Anwen she'd say our intelligence and our capacity for evil."

We laugh 'cause it's true, that's exactly what she would say. "To answer your question though, I think our ability to choose is what makes us human. We can choose to be good, or we can choose to be evil."

This time my eyes widen. This is the first time I've felt like I'm actually a human, at least since I was turned into a monster.

"Why do you ask?"

Should I tell her? Will she understand? The pressure in my head is building up,

"I have Void Magic..." She tilts her head.
"After I came back from treatment, I found out I could use Void Magic."
For the first time in a long time, I let my guard down, "I think I'm a human, I want to be a human, but am I really a person?" It's been so long since I've been able to stop pretending,
"I just pretend to be human but I don't actually know what that's like..."

She takes my hand and squeezes, "I'm not sure I understand, but I don't think that makes you any less human." The pressure starts building and declining at the same time.
"You could've chosen to be mean but instead you choose to bring happiness to others." The pressure alleviates, tears fall from my face. Alice hugs me, "I'm really unsure of how you even managed to get

Void Magic but just because I don't understand doesn't mean you're any less real."

I hug her back and sniffle, "Yeah, I don't know either." She nods. I want to tell her everything but I don't think I can.

She breaks from the hug, nodding and smiling softly, "That sounds really confusing, Emilia."

I nod, "Yeah, I'm confused too." She squeezes my hand again. "I don't even know who I am if I'm not pretending to be human." She lets go of my hand and darts to her feet, hitting her head on the steps with a thud.

I get up and try to check on her, "Oh frick, are you ok?"

Swatting my hands away, she says in a pained tone, "You're you. You are Emilia Jang and you are human. No matter what anyone says." I smile at her, she smiles back.

A robotic voice starts to speak, "You have: Three minutes left. Lightning round, begin."

Alice's gaze meets my own, "'Lightning round'? What does that mean?"

I wince as a loud shriek surrounds the area, "How much do you wanna bet that we're about to find out?" Alice picks up her gun from the floor and I grab her hand.

"We gotta go."

We get out from under the stairs, a blue hologram appears in front of us, accompanied by a voice that says "Two minutes and thirty seconds left." A crash comes from upstairs and I drag Alice past the staircase and out of the house. With my gun in one hand and Alice's hand in my other, we bump into Diana.

"Diana?!" We both exclaim.

She grabs my wrist and starts running, "No talking! Just run!" Chasing us is what appears to be a fish with legs. I try to get a better look at it, it's not that scary to be hone- never mind it has teeth! Its blue scales shimmer in the moonlight. I wonder if those scales are sharp. We weave past rundown house after rundown house until a tunnel enters our line of sight. We run to the tight tunnel to catch our breath. Flinching as the Nightmare that was chasing us gets to the base of the tunnel. The Nightmare starts ramming its head into the base. The ceiling beginning to crack. Alice holds up her gun and shoots it before it can bury us alive. Another thud comes from on top of the tunnel. There's more?! We're about to get buried alive, aren't we. The hologram says only ten seconds remain.

The thuds are getting louder. Just how many of them are trying to kill us? Alice yelps. I take out my gun and shoot the claw that scratched her. She presses her other hand against the wound and winces. Her face turning pale. Of course the Nightmare had to have venomous claws! Everything goes dark.

The robotic voice starts speaking, "Congratulations, you have survived. Your grade on the exam is: A+." Huh?! A+?! I've never gotten a grade that high before! I begin to wake up. I sit up and rub my eyes, trying to take in my surroundings. That's odd, Marion and Ms. Carvenon aren't here.

Anwen, who's beside me is stretching her arms, "Something happened in the simulation and Marion started freaking out. Ms. Carvenon left me and Catarina here to watch over everyone while you guys were still out."

Silvia laughs from behind me, "Marion got what was coming to her. It's not like she has any talent anyways."

Catarina groans from the row beside mine, "I can't believe we got a C- on the exam."

"Yeah, we should've watched where we were going. Tripping and falling is such an idiotic way to almost fail the exam." Anwen sighs. I lean forward to rest on my desk. I can practically feel Silvia's glare.

Diana tries to calm the situation down, "Guys-"

"Are you guys seriously ignoring me?!" Silvia Screeches.

Louis, who's behind Diana apparently dislikes harmony 'cause he says, "Someone's ma-"

"Shut it, Louis!" She exclaims. Why is our teacher never in the classroom for these moments?

Anwen closes her eyes and slumps her shoulders, letting out a heavy sigh, "Silvia, no one wants to hear you talk about how you obviously sabotaged Marion."

She pinches her nose, "Honestly, if I had tangible proof that you did something, I'd immediately tell Ms. Carvenon and get you dropped from the class." I am not turning around, nope, no way.

Silvia scoffs, "They really didn't teach you manners, did they? Isn't it common sense to look at someone when you're talking to them?"

Anwen's jaw tenses, "Why would I, a Lupo, look at someone who clearly doesn't deserve my respect?" I tense up, I look at Catarina without moving my head and she's tensed up too.

"You think you're so great just because you come from a prominent family!" Oh great, Silvia's yelling

Anwen finally turns around and looks at Silvia, her eyes holding a cold glint to it and her mouth twists into a smile, "Yeah, I do actually." Silvia moves to lunge at Anwen.

I guess the whole class is watching now 'cause Louis and Aaron start chanting, "Fight! Fight! Fight!" Anwen shields her face.

A loud scoff comes from the other side of the room before Silvia gets to Anwen, "Imbeciles, all of you. Beek, if you are unable to maintain composure then you have no right to be here. It's unbecoming to disparage a fellow classmate at such a volume." The class goes silent. Does this mean Damon enjoyed Marion's company? I would've never guessed. Marion's a bit annoying but she's nice enough. I would've thought that Damon had found her unbearable. I guess he's nicer than I thought. I do hope Marion's okay though.

The bell rings signalling the end of the day. Do we just get up and leave? Damon gets up, then Aaron, then the rest of the class starts getting ready to leave.

Anwen nudges me, "I'm abducting you today. Let's go." She gets up from her seat and heads to the cubbies.

I laugh, "We should get slushy's on the way back." I skip after her and grab my backpack. She looks at me and grins, we head out of the class.

Lila steps in front of us, "My sister isn't at school today so can I walk home with you guys?" I nod, Anwen furrows her brows. The three of us turn left and walk past Ms. Belkin and Ms. Octinera's class. Making another left, we start heading down the dreaded six flights of stairs. Luckily we got out quickly 'cause the hallways haven't flooded with students yet. Once we're at the bottom we walk towards the office and out of the school. The cool November wind running through our hair. Turning left again, we start walking down the sidewalk.

"I'm surprised things seemed so normal at school, what with Damon being a Nightmare and all." I say.

Anwen hums in acknowledgment, "Mr. Petrova actually has Damon on a tight leash right now. Everyone was really upset about the whole thing especially the higher ups at the Academy, but Mr. Petrova said that 'a child should not be burdened by who their parents are.'" That makes sense, I nod along. The scattered trees around have orange leaves, a reminder at how much time has passed.

"I heard he really advocated for Damon." Lila says. We pass the subway station and head for the crosswalk.

Anwen nods, "He got a lot of sympathy from others who feel like Damon deserves the chance to live a life. I don't think he's going to be able to attend the Academy though." We get to the crosswalk.

Lila nods in agreement, "Alright guys, I gotta go this way." She points left, "It was nice walking with you!" I smile and wave as she turns towards the bank. Anwen raises an eyebrow. We cross the street.

I squint as the sun shines in my eyes and the wind blows against us, "How come Damon won't be able to attend the Academy?" We pass the pizza place and head down the hill to the gas station

She looks up, "According to my dad, it's because the Academy doesn't want to raise a weapon that could turn on them."

Chapter 20

Missing

Amidst the loud chatter, Ms. Carvenon walks to the front of the class, "Children I have two announcements to make." The chatter dies down the second she starts speaking, none of us wanting to get on her bad side.

"Yesterday, during the simulation, something had happened to Marion and so she will no longer be a Reverie in training candidate." Right, Marion wasn't there when I woke up yesterday. I wonder what happened.

"Now, for a more important announcement." I straighten up.

"Lila has gone missing, she didn't make it back home yesterday after school."

My eyes widen, I look at Anwen who's beside me, her eyes are open wide while her hand is covering her mouth. "If any of you know anything, please let me or a trusted adult know." Is that why there were so many cops around?

I raise my hand, "Ms. Carvenon?"

My voice is shaky as I look up and make eye contact with her, "Me and Anwen walked to Block Street with her..."

Ms. Carvenon raises her eyebrows, "Come with me to the office."

We nod and get out of our seats, following her. "You may use the free time to get your homework done." She announces to the class. We pass Alice who gives us a thumbs up and a gentle smile.

We turn right outside the classroom and walk down the steps towards Ms. Akt's class. We walk in silence down the next flight of steps past the gym's mural. We turn left and walk down more steps towards the graduate photo hall. Making one more right till we see the office entrance and walking in.

Ms. Hannah is talking to a police officer before turning to us from behind her desk, "Oh, Hello, girls, Ms. Carvenon. What brings you all down here?"

Anwen looks at the constable, "Is Lila really missing...?"

He crouches down to our level, "Lila never made it home last night, do you girls know anything."

Anwen nods, she seems collected but I can tell she's shaken, "Me and Emilia walked home with her yesterday. I thought it was strange that she wanted to walk with us since she lives in the opposite direction." How could I forget that? Lila DOES live in the opposite direction, so what was she doing with us?

The constable furrows his brows, "She walked home with you two?"

I nod, "Yeah, she ran down Block street afterwards though."

He runs his hands through his hair, "Did you see where she went?" Me and Anwen shake our heads. Lila purposely went down Block Street even though her home is in the opposite direction... Was she meeting someone? If she was, that probably means she was kidnapped.

I gather the courage to speak, "Was she kidnapped?"

The officer's eyes widen and he stiffens up, "That's... one of the avenues we're investigating." Anwen's eyes dart to look at me, though her expression isn't one of surprise. I guess she came to the same conclusion I did.

I start fiddling with my hands, "If Lila was going the opposite direction of her house then she probably had a purpose. She doesn't have an allowance so she couldn't have been trying to buy something and she couldn't have gotten on the subway." The officer listens closely to me.

"That means she was probably meeting someone, which also means she was probably kidnapped..."

He sighs, "That is one of the avenues that we're investigating. More information will be on the news, shortly. As of right now, you girls are the last to see Lila. If you remember anything, please reach out." He gets up and leaves the office.

"You girls stay here, I'll have your parents come pick you up. You won't remember anything in this environment." Ms. Carvenon leads us to the bench and has us sit down before signaling Ms. Hannah and going back to class.

"Anwen, are you alright?" I whisper.

Anwen wraps her arms around herself, "I knew something was wrong. I feel so stupid. How could I not have realized anything sooner?" The only sound in the office is that of Ms. Hannah calling our parents.

"Anastasia would've figured it out..."

"You shouldn't compare yourself to your sister." I respond, still fiddling with my hands.

Anwen scrunches her nose, "Why not? Anastasia is talented, she's powerful, smart, pretty, tall, kind, she's the pride of the Lupo's. If Anastasia were here, Lila wouldn't be missing."

I try to respond but she continues, "Anastasia is perfect... and I'm not." I don't know what to say. How can I comfort her?

"Girls, your parents will be here shortly." Ms. Hannah's voice breaks the silence. We nod to show our acknowledgment.

"Emilia?" My father's voice is soothing, that's new. He rushes towards me, "What happened, are you ok?"

I nod, "Yeah, I'm ok. It's just... Lila went missing."

My dad freezes, "When? Yesterday?"

I nod again, "Me and Anwen were the last people to see her. They want us to go home so we can try to remember something that can help."

He sighs and hugs me, "I'm glad you're okay."

Mrs. Lupo enters the office and does the exact same thing my dad did, "Anwen, you're not hurt are you?"

When Anwen expresses that she's ok, Mrs. Lupo turns to my dad, "Hello, Mr. Jang. What brings you here?" They both get up and my dad whispers something to her, her eyes widen and she looks at Anwen.

My dad walks towards me and takes my hand, "You ready to go?"

I smile, "Yep." We leave the office and go out the main doors to the right. We walk past the yard and head to the car.

He looks down at me and asks, "What happened yesterday?"

Once we're inside the black SUV, I respond, "Lila said she wanted to walk home with me and Anwen, when we got to Block Street we went different ways." I close the door and buckle up my seatbelt.

"Is that all you remember?" He presses.

I look down at my hands and the black car mat, "Yeah, that's all I remember."

He looks back at me from the front seat, "If you remember anything, please tell me. It's important."

I continue looking down, "I know."

My dad hands me an envelope, "Cody sent you a letter." I open the letter and start reading it.

"Dear Emilia,
I heard what happened from dad. I knew you'd be eligible for the Academy. How's your mom doing? How are you finding the training?

You gotta get your heart pumping to get stronger. As for me, I've been doing well. I got a part time job and I'm making some money. Once you enter the Academy, I'll take you to get a familiar. Don't tell dad though.
Good luck
Cody"

"What does it say?" My dad asks

Not wanting my dad to ruin my chances at getting a familiar, I respond, "He's just asking how we're all doing and telling me that I need to move around more to get stronger."

His voice is warm, "That's nice, I'm glad you and Cody get along so well."

~~~~~

A new day. Lila still hasn't been found. A week has passed since she went missing. None of my friends arrived at school yet so I decided to sit on a shady rock in the corner of the yard.

A weight that fills me with dread falls on my shoulders, "You do know she's most definitely dead by now, right?" Yay, me. A. is here with more unwanted commentary.
~~~~~

I sigh, "I know. How could I not?" A group of kids run right past us, not noticing how I'm seemingly talking to nobody.

She laughs, wrapping her arms around me, "That's true, you're quite smart." The bell rings, I shove her off me and start walking towards my grades' line.

Scoffing, I respond, "Stop trying to butter me up. What do you want?"

Following me, she says, "I told you what I want."

"You're gonna have to be patient and wait." I say. I get in line and Ms. Carvenon starts leading us inside. Once we make it to class, I along with my classmates take our seats.

Ms. Carvenon once again walks to the front of the class, "As you know, over the past few days we've had a therapist come to the school so those who need to talk about their feelings regarding Lila may do so between now and lunch." I look at Anwen, she looks back at me. We get up and walk out the classroom

"You look like crap." I tell her as we enter the hallway. The dark bags under her eyes are incredibly noticeable.

"Are you even allowed to say 'crap'?" She smiles. We walk down past Ms. Akt's room.

I smile back at her, "Nope!" Laughter erupts from our chests. I move to hold the railing to steady myself.

As our laughter dies down I continue, "You know it's not your fault she went missing." We continue down the stairs.

Anwen yawns, "Then why do I feel so guilty?" She clearly hasn't been sleeping for a while.

I'm not sure how to respond to that, "You need to rest." We walk past the gym's mural and towards the room the therapist is in.

"I'm gonna use the washroom, go on ahead." She yawns again and goes off. I turn left to enter the washroom. Pushing open the door I freeze. Lila...? What is Lila doing here? In the middle of the washroom, in front of the sink, is Lila. She looks at me, something about her is off.

"Lila? We were looking all over for you! Where were you!" I rush over to her, trying to grab her but the second I blink, she's gone.

The feeling of dread washes over me as A. grabs my hand and smiles down at me, "Do you like it?" My eyes widen, was that just an illusion? What kind of sick joke is this?!

Unable to contain myself, I start whisper-yelling, "You're sick! How could yo-"

She glares at me, "After I gave you Void Magic and saved your life, you call me 'sick'?"

She starts squeezing my hand, "Are you so dull that you can't even recognize your own friend?"

My eyes widen, "What do you mean? What do you mean by that? That's not her! That can't be her!"

Scowling, she continues, "Void Magic gives you the ability to see the dead, remember? You're getting stronger so you're unlocking more and more of your potential. Be grateful you got closure."

I move to slap her, "Grateful?! She's dead!" My hand passes through her.

She grabs me and presses her finger to my forehead, "If it weren't for me, you would be dead! Talk to me with respect or I'll make you." Pain fills my body, I go limp in her hold. It hurts, it hurts, it hurts. It stings and burns and feels like I'm being ripped apart. I can't breathe! The pain stops. I collapse to the floor, panting heavily. I can't get enough oxygen. I glare at her and she just smiles.

Chapter 21

The sting of a jellyfish courses through my hands, "OW! That hurts!" I let go of Cate's hair and hold my palm. Mari comes up from behind me and kicks the back of my knees. Cate dodges my flailing self as I yelp and fall face first into the snow.

Cate rushes towards me, "Millie! Are you okay?"

I get up and rub the snow off myself, "Mari, that's cheating!" I tackle her to the ground, Cate tries to pull me off her. She's laughing so hard I don't think she's breathing.

A scoff comes from behind us, "Ugh, how juvenile." I freeze for a second only for Mari to shove me off her with ease. The cold winter air rushes past us. I turn to face Damon. Who else would scoff like that but him?

I make eye contact with him then immediately look away because eye contact is gross, "We're ten, we're allowed to act like kids. Plus, we're just training." He rolls his eyes.

A familiar mocking voice butts in, "I told you she was a know-it-all." Oh great, Silvia is here too. Kaine is beside her with her hands in the pockets of her dark coat.

I ignore them and continue, "Who even let you guys out? Didn't you guys get the newsletter a while ago warning us to not go out alone?"

"Says the group who's also alone." Silvia responds. Damon facepalms.

Cate pipes up, "Actually, Mrs. Abdul is over there on the bench." He points to Mari's mom who, as stated, is sitting a little bit away from us on one of the benches.

Silvia turns red, "Yeah, well-!"

Damon glares at her, "If you're going to screech at unholy volumes, at least be fundamentally correct." She narrows her gaze at him and sneers. Kaine on the other hand looks the other way, trembling slightly. I assume she's trying not to laugh. She always did find it funny when people humbled Silvia. Silvia storms off in the other direction, Kaine follows. Damon on the other hand groans and drags his feet in her direction. I guess he wasn't allowed out unless he went in a group. Snowflakes start falling from the sky. Mari's mom calls for us so we can start going back. We make our way towards her as she starts walking towards the entrance of the park.

"Lila loved the snow..." I mutter. A., who's behind me smiles wide.

Mari tilts her head, "Don't you mean 'loves'? She hasn't been found yet so we don't know if she's dead or not."

"Actually, in most child abduction cases it is imperative to find the missing person within twenty-four hours of said abduction." Cate rambles. Mari's face falls upon hearing that. I guess she just put two and two together.

"It would be statistically improbable to assume that Lila is still alive." His face falls, probably realizing that this isn't a great time to go on a rant.

We catch up to Mari's mom and start heading back to their house. Passing by the houses of some of our peers. The frost biting my nose, I lose balance for a second. I absolutely love it when I almost slip and die on ice. "Did you kids have fun?" Mari's mom asks. We give her a thumbs up.

"I'm glad." She responds

Once we get to Mari's street, she yells, "Race ya home!" She bolts down the street, I chase after her and Cate chases after me.

Surprisingly, I'm faster than him. Either that, or he's letting me win. A yelp comes from behind me and the next thing I know, my forehead hits the icy, salt covered sidewalk. Mari stops and turns back to look at us, she starts cackling. Cate groans and gets off me. I push myself off the ground. The spot my forehead hit covered in crimson.

"Emilia, Cato, are you both ok?" Mari's mom rushed to crouch down near us. We both nod, blood dripping down my face. She smiles a broken smile, clearly unnerved by my probably incredibly bloody face. She helps us up and walks with us over to the house. My face is both hot and cold at the same time. Walking up the lawn, we finally catch up to Mari who's sitting on the porch.

She sticks her tongue out at us, "I win!"

Her mother sighs and flicks Mari's forehead, "I told you to stop running in the winter."

Mari whines, "But how else can I prove I'm better than everyone?"

Mari's mom flicks her again, "You're not special for winning a game you blindsided others into playing." She then unlocks the door and lets us inside. I walk inside, my head throbbing as I start taking off my coat, sweater and boots. Cate does the same. Mari's mom takes me up the spruce wood stairs and to the washroom. I sit on the bathtub ledge and grab a wet wipe. I take the wipe and start wiping the blood off my face. I look down at the wipe, red covers most of its surface. She grabs some iodine and cotton balls, drenching the cotton in the antiseptic and dabbing it on my forehead. I flinch from the cold before relaxing.

She finishes disinfecting my forehead, "All set, you can go and play now."

I smile at her, "Thank you!"

Mari pops her head in the washroom, "You done?" I nod and head over to her.

"Let's play house!" She exclaims. She drags me to her room where Cate is already waiting.

"I'll be the mom and Mimi can be the dad!"

"What about me?" Cate asks.

Mari looks up in thought, "You're gonna be our kid."

Cate pouts, "Why can't you be the kid?"

"You want to be the mom?" Mari asks.

He hesitates for a second before responding, "No..."

"Then you're gonna be Mimi's child!" Mari says delightedly.

How do I make this more fun? I exclaim "Oh, OH! What if Cate is my kid but not your kid so like I cheated on you?!" Cate's eyes widen with horror.

Mari's eyes widen with joy, "OH! And what if I'm like super upset about it and I slap you?!"

Mari's pink duvet creases as Cate gets up from the bed, eyes darting down at us, "The probability of Millie getting hurt again is quite high."

"Hmmm, that's true. I don't want you to get in trouble, Mari."

I turn to her, looking up as I try to think about the consequences Mari might face. "OH! Maybe I can hit you back!"

"YEAH! Let's do that!" She exclaims.

"...Can't we play a normal, happy family?" Cate says hesitantly.

Me and Mari turn towards him, "No."

~~~~~
~~~~~

Seventeen days pass by, seventeen more days since Lila went missing. "Aemas came so fast this year. Don't you think, Emilia?" My mom asks. My moms side of the family is chatting in the dining room about whatever politics they think is interesting. I nod and grab my food, going past my mom to join my cousins at the kids table.

As I sit down beside Wren, Rowan looks at Finny and says, "Do you think I have double strength in my arm?"

Finny's eyes light up, "Wanna test it ou-"

I sigh and lean back on the brown couch "You guys aren't gonna start smacking each other are you?"

Finny and Rowan look away, "No..." They definitely were.

Wren giggles, "They definitely were."

I look at my second and third oldest cousins, "And how exactly do you guys think that's gonna turn out?"

"I think it'd turn out great." Finny says

"Yeah, I think it'd be fun." Rowan agrees.

Wren looks up at me, "Can't they just go in the backyard and fight each other there?"

Violet responds, "Do you want someone to end up in the hospita-?"

"Yes." Wren interrupts.

I stand up and move to block the door behind us, "No one is fighting anyone or going to the hospital. Can't we all just eat dinner and relax?"

"Ok, then can we race instead?" Finny proposes.

I move away from the door and groan, "Fine, you guys can run around the alleyway behind the house." I guess I'm on 'tell the adults' duty.

"I bet I'm faster than you, Rowan! I outran a tornado during the tornado warning at school." WHAT?!
We all pause before he continues, "What?"

I hesitate to respond, mainly because I know the answer is going to be awful, "Okay, now hold on, what do you mean by 'I outran a tornado'?"

He smiles, "I was in the washroom when the tornado warning happened so I went home." EXCUSE ME?!

My eyes are nearly popping out of their sockets, "You did what?!"

Violet sighs and looks away, "I told him not to do that..." Wren starts laughing.

Rowan furrows his brows, "How are you not dead?"

"I told you, I outran the tornado." Finny says as if it's the most obvious thing.

I sigh, "There's no way the tornado was even near you or you'd be dead." I wonder if Tia Salma knows about this.

Finny responds cockily, "It was close, the air around tornadoes are localized so I was fine. Even if it was closer, I could just run in the opposite direction around it and it would disappear." I don't even know what to say to that. Is he stupid? I think he's stupid.

"Ya know what? You guys just go and race." I open the door for them. The frigid air rushes in. My cousins get their winter gear on and run past the gate.

Violet stops beside me, "One of them is gonna get a concussion."

"Probably." I respond.

"Shouldn't you stop them?" Violet looks up at me.

I walk to the coat rack and put on my sweater, coat and boots before walking out the door, "Eh, it's not my problem." Me and Violet walk down the path in the backyard and passed the fence. Finny and Rowan are in their ready position. Wren blows a whistle and the two boys bolt down the alley. Where she got a whistle from, nobody knows. As they run down the dark alley, Finny slips and falls face first into the ice while Rowan runs ahead.

Violet leisurely heads towards her brother, "Faster than a tornado, huh?"

"Shut up, Violet." Finny groans, pushing himself off the ground. I look behind me to see Wren videotaping the whole thing on her camera with a large smile on her face.

Rowan jogs back over to us, "I won!" We all head back inside, walking through the pathway into my backyard and into the house. Finny goes to tell Tia Danna he ate dirt. I doubt she'll be very surprised though considering that's just a normal Tuesday for them.

Chapter 22

With winter break ending, we can finally get started with poisons class! I walk into class with my head held high. Now that I'm eleven I have one up on Damon. I'm better at magic AND older than him? He'll obviously have to acknowledge that he's not all that. I walk past him to my desk, sitting down.

I turn back to see Diana arrived before me, "Happy belated birthday!" I grin at her.

She smiles back, "You too! I can't believe we're finally eleven." I nod and she continues, "We're pretty much halfway done the school year. In June we'll find out who gets to go to the Academy."

"Emilia! Diana! Happy belated birthday!" Alice walks into the class all chipper. Me and Diana turn to face her.

"Thank you!" I respond.

"Thanks, Alice. Happy New Year too." Diana says after me. Alice goes to sit at her desk.

Oh right, New Years passed, "Happy new year, guys!" The bell rings and rapid footsteps can be heard from the hall.

Catarina rushes in while panting, "Happy New Year" She passes by Alice's desk and sits in her own, looking at me and Diana, "Happy late Birthday to you two."

I try to listen for Anwen's footsteps which is unfortunately very difficult because apparently everyone decided to get to class like now, "Alice, is Anwen coming to school today?" She opens her mouth to speak but the national anthem starts playing. Groans come from the hall from the kids who didn't make it to class. The joys of it being too cold to stay outside is we don't have to line up.

Me and my classmates stand up and Alice mouths, "Dentist." I guess Anwen is getting her teeth cleaned or something. Once the national anthem is over we sit down in our seats. Cameron and Louis start talking about who knows what and Ms. Carvenon loudly clears her throat.

Our principal, Mr. Norris, starts saying the day's announcements, "First of all, I'd like to welcome you all back to school after the winter break. It's been a long time but I hope each and every one of you is ready to be back to working hard." I roll my eyes, Mr. Norris is such a weirdo. I mean, he has a wife and he's in love with Aaron's mom.

"And a happy birthday to Diana Zelinski who's birthday was on the second. Lastly, happy birthday to both Emilia Jang and Damon Petrova who were born on the fifth." ...WHAT?! I whip my head to the right, making eye contact with Damon. His eyes are wide. His face contorts to a nasty scowl and I glare at him. There is NO way we share a birthday! With my luck he's probably OLDER than me too! Ugh! Why did I have to be born in the evening?

"Alright class, we're doing something a little different today." As Ms. Carvenon speaks, our heads turn towards her as she walks past that twat, Damon, to the front of the classroom.

"Since poison is a subject that requires a lot of care, we will be starting now rather than later." Aw no, Anwen's gonna miss some of it. Wait... she probably already knows a lot about poisons since she's been trying to build immunity. I know it's a useful skill to have but isn't it scary to eat poison?

"You'll be put into groups of three, one group will have four members." Please let me not get put with Damon.

"Marin, you will be with Louis, Catarina and Kala." That's unfortunate. Mari will be lucky if she doesn't get poisoned today.

"Kaine will be with Silvia and Diana." Yippee! I'm not with Silvia! I'm probably getting put with Damon, aren't I?

"Aaron will be with Anwen and Max." Crap, I'm with Damon...

"Lastly Damon will be with Alice and Emilia." I mean, at least I'm with Alice. Everyone stays silent, it seems like most of us are unhappy with our group mates. Why we couldn't pick who to work with, I don't know.

"Well? You children are in grade 5, take some initiative." I look at Alice and she shrugs.

"It doesn't matter how you do it, just go and sit in your groups." Everyone starts getting up from their seats. The sound of desks being dragged across the floor fill the room. I grimace from the screeching of the desks scraping across the tile floor. Alice gets up from her desk and sits in Anwen's seat, beside mine. Damon, at the other end of the classroom, drags his feet as he walks towards us, scowling as usual. Me and Alice get up and shift the desks to face Diana's desk. Silvia brought hers with her, clearly not wanting us to use it.

"It appears as though we have a mutual date of birth." Damon says with as much enthusiasm as a dead squid.

"What time increment were you born?"

Here goes nothing, the moment of truth, "Seven in the evening"

Damon grins, "One in the afternoon."

Alice tilts her head and looks at Damon, "Didn't you live in the Nightmare Territory? That's close-ish to Honolulu and I don't think we're in the same timezone as them." Mine and Damon's eyes widen, our stupid selves forgot to factor in timezones.

I grin, "Since we don't have much information on Nightmare territory, we can use Honolulu as a reference."

I look at Damon, "What time-"

"It should not take this long for you all to get in your groups." Ms. Carvenon states from her desk.

Damon sits down at Diana's desk and grumbles, "It's the same time..." No...no no no no no no no! There's no way!

"What do you mean, 'It's the same time.'?" My voice quivers as I ask.

Damon rolls his eyes, "Are you dense? We were born at the same time. One in the afternoon and seven in the evening are the same time given our locations at birth." I slump on my desk. This cannot be happening. Damon crosses his arms and looks to his right.

Alice laughs awkwardly, "That just means we're more of a team than we thought." How are you gonna convince us if you can't even convince yourself?

"Maybe we can have a competition...?"

Me and Damon perk up, "Competition?"

Alice responds, "Uh... Yeah! Whoever gets the better mark in this class wins!"

"Deal!" We both exclaim.

"I do hope you two are going to behave today." Our teacher remarks. Obviously she had to be standing behind me as we did that.
"Since you both are SO enthusiastic about poisons class, I'm sure you wouldn't mind showing me which of these items" she gestures to a table at the front that has all sorts of vials on it, "is poison and which are not"

"May I smell them?" Damon asks, not missing a beat.

Ms. Carvenon looks shocked, "As long as you don't consume anything." Damon starts opening smelling the vials before closing them and putting them back.

He starts pointing at each vial and naming them, "Nightshade, foxglove, belladonna, oleander, hemlock par-"

"I'm not sure how you identified each of them but regardless, you get full marks."
Ms. Carvenon then turns to me, "Emilia, what do each of these poisons do to the body?"

Crap, "Um... they shut the body down?"

"How?" She responds. Damon grins from behind her.

I respond, sounding as confident as I can, "By causing your body to stop living."

Ms. Carvenon sighs, "Zero marks."
She looks at me then Damon, "Both of you, go back to your seats." Me and Damon walk back to our seats and sit down.
"I will be handing out the poisons so you may familiarize yourselves with them. Do NOT put the contents in anyone's mouth." She starts handing out the vials to our grouped desks, one by one.
The sound of coughing can be heard, "Aaron Bellamy! What do you think you're doing?!" A crash echoes through the room. The entire class looks in our teacher's direction, then at Aaron.

"Did he just poison Max...?" Alice mutters. I look down at the broken vial, there's nothing on the floor but glass shards. Well, rest in peace I guess? The coughing continues. He's not ACTUALLY gonna die is he?

"Idiots..." Damon says under his breath.

Ms. Carvenon helps Max up and walks towards the door, "Aaron, needless to say you'll be in detention and your parents will be called. Come with me to the office. Bring your bag, you will not be going to the Academy." Aaron's eyes widen and Max continues to cough. They leave the classroom in a hurry with Aaron looking like someone just slapped him. I don't know what he expected. You can't just poison people. The class erupts with chatter. Lila already went missing and is likely dead, isn't it kinda bad to try and kill your classmate so soon after one went missing? I will never understand people. I glance at the empty desks, Marion, Lila and Cameron's. I mean, Cameron deserved to get kicked. Like, who tries to shoot other people? Even if the bullets were rubber, that can seriously hurt someone. There's Marion, who was most definitely sabotaged by Silvia. Then there's Lila, she didn't deserve what happened to her. I doubt she would've become a Reverie but that doesn't mean her life is worthless.

"I wonder if we'll ever find Lila." I look up to see Alice looking at the empty desks.

"Yeah... I hope we do. Her family deserves to know what happened to her. Not knowing is the worst." I respond and Alice nods

Damon looks at the empty desks too, "Lila was the blonde girl with bangs, correct?"

He actually remembered? "Wow, I can't believe you actually remembered. I figured you thought we're all beneath you."

Damon rolls his eyes, "You ARE beneath me, I just have a good memory."

"Keep telling yourself that." I stick my tongue out at him.

"I am the pinnacle of this class." He scowls.

"Guys?" Alice chimes in.

I laugh, "Oh really? Then why am I better at magic than you?"

"Yet you couldn't beat me during our fight." He sneers.

"You didn't beat me either." I fire back.

"Guys!" Alice interrupts us. "Can't we all be friends?"

"No." Me and Damon say in unison.

"Why would I wanna be friends with this jerk?" I respond.

"Why would I wish to align myself with someone incompetent." Damon glares at me.

I cough, "More competent than you apparently." Damon seethes while Alice just laughs awkwardly.

"Uh, Do you know where my desk is?" I jolt and turn to see Anwen standing behind me.

I look around the classroom at all the empty desks, "To be honest, I'm not exactly sure."

Damon looks at Anwen, "Lupo, my step mother says your family is coming over for dinner. Ensure your sister does not boil us all to death."

She smiles her 'I'm gonna throttle this kid' smile, "Anastasia is not some rabid dog, Petrova."

"You guys are having dinner tonight?" I tilt my head.

Anwen nods, "All of Team Tyche is gonna be there along with their kids. Damon escaped the last time so this time my parents put me on babysitting duty."

"I don't see why I need a babysitter." He grumbles.

"Who else is gonna be there?" I wonder aloud.

"The Chevalier's along with my aunt and cousin." He responds.

"I don't know whether I prefer being Severus's babysitter or Damon's babysitter." Anwen sighs.

Alice joins in, "What's wrong with Severus? My friend who goes to Runnymede says he's really reserved."

Damon scoffs, "He's nothing but a spineless fool."

"Severus is...yeah... he's kinda spineless. He's also really afraid of me for some reason." Anwen adds.

"You'd think his mother would be more tolerable but she's not. Something about her is wrong, off putting." Damon mutters. Off Putting? I wonder why.
He turns to me, "You'll understand when you meet her." Well that's scary. I don't know if I want to meet her anymore.

Chapter 23

Part-Dragon

Ms. Carvenon walks to the front of the classroom, "As you all know, today you'll be doing another simulation. What makes today different from the previous simulations is that I'll be adjusting the settings to not block any pain out for you." This is terrible. I knew it felt different when I scraped my knee last time! I chalked it up to the venom that entered my system. That stuff made everything feel numb. Maybe it was both?

"Um... just to confirm, the pain we felt the previous times WASN'T the full amount?" Kala asks hesitantly.

Ms. Carvenon nods, "That is correct." The class groans. "How do you expect to become a Reverie if you don't learn how to tolerate pain? Pain tolerance is often the difference between life and death." She starts passing the ECG looking stickers around. One by one my classmates place them on their necks. She gets to me.

"Thank you" I say. She nods. I place the sticker on my neck. Bringing my arms to fold onto the desk, I lower my head to rest against them. Closing my eyes, I hear rustling and footsteps. The sound of Louis saying who knows what causing Ms. Carvenon to shush him. Dark. It all goes dark.

The same robotic voice from before starts talking, "Simulation Round: Hide and Seek." Yippee! I'm great at hide and seek!

"First and only rule, exiting the building is prohibited, doing so will result in a failing grade." Huh?

"Good luck" Walls start materializing around me. I tap my foot against the white tile floor. I think I'm in an office building. Looking down at my outfit, I'm wearing the same thing I wore to school today. No weapons on me this time. I wince as the sun shines through the windows that cover the outer walls of the room. Desks and computers start appearing around me. I should probably check how many floors there are. I walk towards the glass, the ground seems to be really far down so I must be near the top. Pressing myself against the glass, I look up. The building stretches higher than I can see, way past the clouds. Footsteps echo through the hallway outside. Dark wavy hair comes into my view.

Is that...? "Catarina?"

Catarina turns her head, "Oh thank God you're here." She smiles and runs up to me.

"I should be saying that to you." I smile back and we both laugh.

"We probably won't need to worry about the seeker for a while since it's on the lower floors and working its way up." She says.

I tilt my head, "How-"

She grins, "My Specialty Magic. I sent part of my soul into one of the computers in the room I started in and it looks like they're connected to what Ms. Carvenon uses to start the simulation. I saw how much longer we have and where the seeker is as well as a blueprint of the building."

I really got lucky running into her, "Do you know what the seeker is?"

She nods, "It's a Calibre four, Spawned Type Nightmare. As for what it looks like, all I know is that it's part dragon." We're screwed.

We're gonna fail, "Oh lovely. We might have to fight a dragon-"

She interrupts, "Part dragon"

I sigh, "We might have to fight a part dragon Nightmare and we don't have any weapons on us." A loud roar causes the building to shake.
I look at Catarina with wide eyes, "That doesn't sound like just a 'part dragon.'"

She shrugs, "Let's try to go to the higher floors. The Nightmare is searching each floor one by one. We won't be able to get the bonus marks but it's better than failing."

"Bonus marks?" There are bonus marks?

She nods, "Yeah, whoever can defeat the Nightmare will get bonus marks." Oh that's tempting.
 "Alice was with me when we started and she went off to defeat the Nightmare." I look up. If Alice is trying to defeat it then maybe I can give her a hand and we both get the bonus marks... hmm...

I turn to Catarina, "You can go up, I'm gonna go find Alice."

Her eyes widen, "Huh?!"

"Go find Anwen, if the Nightmare is Calibre four, Anwen won't stand a chance against it." I start heading past the computers and towards the entryway.
 "Good luck!" I wave at her then I start looking for the stairway. The hallway is what you would expect from an office building. The walls tremble. Everything looks the same. I make it to the staircase. Opening the door, I look down the centre. That is...A LOT of stairs. The concrete stairs wrap around the perimeter of the stairwell. Hmm, Oppa said our threads are pretty strong. Are they strong enough to

hold my body weight? Oh well, one way to find out! Amethyst threads materialize from my fingertips and wrap around the railing on the floor above me. I tug on the threads and look down the center of the stairs. This is a horrible idea. I shorten the threads length and pull my legs up so my feet aren't touching the stairs. Ok, this seems safe enough. Rocking myself back and forth, I start gaining momentum. I get over the railing on my floor and look down. Never mind, this is a horrible idea. I close my hand around the threads and make the threads lower me down.

"Wait... I didn't ask what floor the Nightmare is on..." My voice echoes slightly. The building trembles once more. A crash echoes the stairwell and something large clacks onto the bottom floor. Is that a door that just fell? I continue lowering myself down, my face beginning to get wet. Oh great, I'm sweating. Wait...heat is supposed to rise so why is it getting hotter the more- oh right, part dragon. Blue fire shoots towards the wall on the floor below me. I guess I found the dragon... part dragon. Rocking myself back and forth again I leap onto the stairs. I'm a floor above the part dragon, now what? Looking over the railing I see it, it's built like a Komodo dragon but much bigger and with wings. Guess getting bit is out of the question. Its sockets are empty, looks like Alice got it pretty good, there's no way it's able to see. A gust of wind flows through the stairway.

"Alice?! You there?!" I call out, my voice echoing more than before.

"Emilia?!" Alice responds. The stairwell gets hotter and brighter again. Alice comes into my line of sight, she dodges the flames mid-air. We make eye contact and she walks on over to me using air magic. Thank heavens she's coming closer, it's harder to understand someone when there's so much echoing.

"Air magic is pretty handy" I smile at her.

She nods and winces, "I guess you came to help me beat the dragon?" Her pants are ripped right above the knee, it looks like the Nightmare bit her.

"Part dragon."
I respond, "Also yeah I am." The Nightmare roars, breaking the railing on the floor below.
"Uh, ok. Quickly, what's the plan?" The Nightmare starts to fly.

"I can suffocate it if you can hold it still. If I'm gonna pass this class I can't let the poison kill me." She says. The dragon shoots fire at us. Me and Alice dart in opposite directions. I go up the stairs and Alice goes down. If I can get on top of the dragon I won't need to tie it up one or two threads at a time. I look back at Alice, she's bleeding a lot. We need to end this quickly.
Alice shouts, "I'll distract it!" As she allows me to enter the Nightmares blind spot, I get my threads to lift me up from three floors

above. Well, here goes nothing. Just do it like Oppa does. I fling myself into the air. Now that I have a better view, I manipulate my threads to tie onto the Nightmare at several points and then onto the various railings. It roars and struggles but it's unable to move for the most part. I reattach myself to a railing and watch as Alice starts using her air magic to suffocate the Nightmare.

The robotic voice from earlier starts talking, "Simulation round will end in: ten seconds." The Nightmare starts thrashing more violently.

"Eight seconds." I attach more threads to it.

"Six seconds" Its tail whacks me in the stomach.

"Four seconds." I crash into the wall and hit my head.

"Two seconds." Everything hurts. I can't breathe. My head is wet.

"Simulation round: over. You will now wake up." My eyes jolt open and I gasp. My breaths are deep and uneven. I'm not in pain anymore. I look at Alice who's also gasping for air. Makes sense since it looked like she was bleeding a lot.

The class starts waking up one by one. Ms. Carvenon walks up between my and Alice's desks, "Good job, girls, I wasn't expecting anyone to be able to defeat the Nightmare. You both get full marks." She smiles at us. We're both still trying to catch our breath.

She walks back to her desk, "You'll all be getting your marks tomorrow. For now, since the simulation ended early, you may work on any outstanding work." Chatter fills the room. Ms. Carvenon must be in a good mood today because she's not saying anything about the noise.

A groan comes from beside me, "I didn't even get to see the Nightmare."

I look at Anwen, "Trust me, you did not want to fight it."

"Getting bit by it was NOT fun." Alice chimes in. I smile at her and she smiles back.

"We make a pretty good team." I say, leaning back on my desk.

Alice gives me a thumbs up, "Heck yeah we are!"

"To be fair, with Emilia's Specialty Magic, she's a pretty good match with anyone." Catarina says thoughtfully.

Silvia laughs, "Except for Damon, clearly."

"You don't get along with Damon either." I retort.

"At least I'm not a know-it-all." She scoffs. Catarina looks away.

Anwen rolls her eyes, "You would say that wouldn't you?"

"What's that supposed to mean?" She asks.

Anwen moves to speak but I do instead, "I'm not taking criticism from someone who thinks the radiation from a microwave will turn you into a Chernobyl catfish."

Diana forces a laugh, "Can't we all just get along?

Alice retorts, "Silvia's been acting like a jerk for way too long, I'm sick of it. Before it was tolerable but since September it's been awful."
Silvia moves to speak but Alice looks at her and continues, "You literally hit your mom and you act like a spoiled brat. You don't live 'in the hood,' you live right across from Anwen."

"Alice, that's too harsh!" Diana says.

Anwen chimes in, "No, Alice is right. We don't live in the hood for one and Silvia buys hundreds of dollars worth of useless junk online per month then claims her mom financially neglects her. To be honest I'm also sick of her constant lies and insults." Silvia gives us two middle fingers and gets on her phone. She's one of the only kids in the grade with a phone. Not to mention she got the newest version the day it came out. I sigh, this is gonna be a long 5 months.

Chapter 24

Ms. Carvenon, with her very...confident voice, starts speaking, "Today's simulation will be one that will test your endurance, thinking skills and magical abilities." I look around to see half the class falling asleep.

"There will be twelve Nightmares in total. One per each of you. The Nightmare assigned to you will stop at nothing to take you out. To make it easier for you all, the only Nightmare you have to worry about is the one assigned to you. The other Nightmares will not go after you." While this seems easy enough, I feel like it's gonna be a lot harder than she's letting on.

"Any questions?" A few people raise their hands.

She sighs, "Yes, Diana?"

Diana puts her hand down, "Is there anything special about the Nightmares that're assigned to each of us?"

"Each Nightmare is tailor made to be your perfect opposition." Our teacher explains. Oh great, I'm gonna die. My classmates jaws slacken as they stare at our teacher with disbelief. She starts passing along the stickers, one by one we place them on our necks and soon enough, we're in the simulation.

The same robotic voice as always starts to speak, "Simulation: Start." Dark walls surround me. Looking down, I notice my clothing. The texture is smooth against my skin but it feels durable. My Nightmare is probably going to fight more physically rather than use magic. It'll probably be built for endurance too. A loud crash coming from further down the hallway can be heard. I think the best solution would be to find someone I can partner up with and then have them beat my Nightmare while I beat theirs. Bolting towards the area of the crash, I start wondering who exactly- I crash into a vase which cracks and breaks on my forehead. OW Ow ow ow ow ow ow ow! My vision, blurry.

Something's running towards me, and it's very large. I roll away from the spot I fell. My sight starts to return. Looking up at what pushed me, I see it, a chimera. Well, this might as well happen. I get up from the floor and start running, quickly losing stamina. Lucky for me, my forehead is also bleeding so I can't even try to hide from it. It hurts SO much! It's throbbing and I can feel the blood oozing from my wound. I wipe my eyes to keep the blood from getting in. Another crash, but this time, it's closer. I turn the corner to see Damon embedded into the wall. Where is his opponent? He groans and gets back on his feet, we make eye contact.

My lungs are burning but I've only been running for a short time, despite that I shout, "I'll take yours so you take mine, 'kay?!" I stop running, heaving beside him. He scowls but reluctantly nods. He points to what looks to be a firefly near the ceiling. A fairy? Well, I guess it just looks like a fairy. Either way, I got this. The chimera stalks towards me to which Damon darts towards it. I- He's gonna die. I wipe my eyes again, trying to get the blood out. Ok, let's do this. I wanna get out and not be in moderate pain anymore. My threads quickly attach to the fairy. It waves its wand. The air gets knocked out of me as I get flung five centimetres into the wall. It flings me again, and again, and again. A roar comes from the chimera. My head hurts, I can't breathe, everything's getting fuzzy. I can't use Aether Magic either 'cause then Damon will definitely notice... I guess I just gotta deal with it, I can't be a strong Reverie like Oppa if I can't handle at least this much. As it moves to fling me again, I yank the threads attached to the fairy. Using my other hand I yank again, then again, then again. The fairy waves its wand, clearly panicking but I just keep pulling it closer to me. Once it's close enough, I grab the fairy and crush it. I fall to the ground. Please tell me Damon isn't losing. Woah, never thought I'd say that. I'm panting like a dog but honestly, it feels nice knowing I beat something Damon couldn't. I look over at him. The chimera is...losing? It's backing away from Damon and snarling like a cornered cat. Damon on the other hand, has dark welts all over his arms but strangely none on the rest of him. I mean, he's still bleeding but who is this guy? He rushes at the chimera and punches it square in the nose. I wince. That must hurt. He jumps onto the chimera and places his hands by the chimera's eyes. Anastasia told us that's how you gouge out someone's eyes. I look away. I really don't wanna see him do that. The chimera roars and there's a squelching sound before a thud and footsteps.

He sits beside me, "Your way of showing gratitude is lacking." This jerk!

I gasp out, "So is yours." I look at him, my nose scrunched.

"...I acknowledge that you have helped me." He says.

I narrow my eyes, "Is that supposed to be your way of saying 'thank you'?"

He rolls his eyes, "Don't be ungrateful."

If I could move I would punch him, "Thanks, I guess." The sounds of thuds and yelling can be heard throughout the building but neither of us move.

"No one seems to like me very much." He mutters.

That's...weirdly vulnerable of him, "Yeah, I wonder why?"

He scoffs, "Your personality isn't very agreeable either." He nudges me.

I hiss and nudge him back harder, "Says the ugly jerk face."

He shoves me, "Decrepit rat!"

I get up and grab his hair by the roots, "I bet your parents change the subject when you come up!"

He glares at me and knees me in the stomach, "Everyone who claims to love you is stating falsehoods!"

I cough and yank his hair, "Worthless jerk!"

He grabs my hair, "Filthy trollop!"

No idea what that means but it sounds mean, "Mouse sized freak!"

"Ugly wench!" He kicks me.

We continue like this for a while before the robotic voice speaks up, "Simulation: complete." I open my eyes and take a long breath.

Ms. Carvenon is standing in front of the room with a displeased look, "There is five minutes until the bell rings. Frankly, I am quite disappointed at the amount of you that failed today. You are dismissed." She walks back to her desk. One by one, we all get up and head to our cubbies. Anwen zooms out of class. Anastasia got some time off so she's coming to pick her up. Mom said I'm going to Cate's home today. I should hurry so I don't keep him waiting. I walk out of class with my backpack.

Alice runs up to me, "That was too easy!"

I laugh, "No! It was awful."

"I think mine got mixed up with someone else's 'cause I was just able to chill on one of the chandeliers the entire time." She smiles.

"Lucky!" Diana shouts from behind us.

Catarina smiles softly, "Yeah, that's really lucky, Alice"

I tilt my head, "Is everything ok, Catarina?" We turn the corner to start heading down the six flights of stairs.

She sighs, "Yeah, I just...don't know if I want to be a Reverie anymore."

Alice responds, "Why not?"

Catarina hesitates, "...I just don't think I can do it. Every class I feel completely outmatched. I'm barely keeping up. I don't think it's for me."

"That's fine, Catarina. Not everyone is a natural at these things. I mean, I'm only in this class because I wanted to see what it's like. I don't actually want to be a Reverie." Diana places a hand on Catarina's shoulder. We continue down the stairs.

Catarina looks down, "I want to leave the class but I don't want to be a failure. I mean, my parents and sister were so excited for me..."

I smile at her, "But in the end, it's your life, right? If you really feel like it's not right for you then you should leave." She looks down at me.

"You don't want to end up in a career you hate. Plus, people who graduate from the academy can't really get other jobs."

We make it to the ground floor, "Anyways, I gotta go but you should think about what YOU want. Bye!" I run off towards the exit. Pushing past the doors I see Cate waiting for me by the fence. I guess his mom sent him to get me since he went home early due to a doctor's appointment.

I walk up to him, "Cate! Guess what?"

He turns around and smiles at me, "What?"

I stand up straighter, "I put on sunscreen today!"

"You're supposed to put on sunscreen every day. Even short exposures to UV radiation can harm your skin's DNA, remember?"

I pout, "I know…"

He laughs, "Come on, let's go" we begin walking north. Anwen and her sister, Anastasia are walking towards us, I wave at them. They smile and wave back before Anastasia's face contorts into a serious look. She tugs Anwen to move faster.

"Emilia, Cato, How are you? I didn't know your dad got off work this early." Anastasia says loudly, she's gripping something in her pocket. Our eyes widen and we turn around to see someone following us. The person stops right in their tracks and vanishes without a trace.

She sighs, and takes out her phone, "That was close, You guys shouldn't be walking alone, let's go to my house. Cato I can ask my dad to call your parents to let them know. I just don't think you both should be alone." We nod and start walking with them.

Cate responds, "Thank you, I didn't even notice there was someone pursuing me."

Anwen grins, "Of course she noticed, Anastasia is at the top of her class and she's our family's pride and joy. It's only natural that she notices when something's wrong."

Anastasia grins and hugs Anwen, "That's cute but you're not getting my magic stones." Anwen scrunches her nose. Me and Cate laugh.

"Although she is right. It's only natural I notice when someone has absolutely no aura."

"The person following us had no aura?" Cate asks. We pass the school and start heading towards Block Street.

Anastasia nods, "That person has zero presence. Only people who have nefarious intentions hide their presence like that."

Wait, that doesn't make sense, "But isn't hiding yourself like that a really advanced skill?"

Anastasia gives me a thumbs up, "Bingo, that's why I was so concerned. Although you both didn't react how I wanted you to. Concealing yourself like that is extremely advanced."

"It's a skill that only people able to beat Calibre ten Nightmares can typically use." Anwen pipes up. Me and Cate tense up.

"So, whatever was following us must've been really dangerous." I mutter.

"Extremely so. I don't think I could've beaten them."

Anastasia smiles, "I definitely would've tried though! I can't let the younger generation die off before they reach their potential. Plus, it's my job as a Lupo to protect people." She's so cool!

Chapter 25

I turn to Cate who's sitting on my chair, "Guess what?"

He looks up from his book, "Millie, with the path your life has been going down, it's safe to say I have no clue what's up." Should I be offended by that?

I grin and flop on my bed, "We have three months left of school!" The light from the window making my room brighter.

"Oh thank god." He says. I sit up and tilt my head.
 "Millie, every time you say 'guess what?' it's either incredibly mundane or you end up telling me you're injured."

"That's not true." I whine.

His mouth forms a line, "The last time you asked me that question you ended up falling halfway down the stairs. The time before you fell up the stairs and scraped your whole knee, the time before that you burnt your hand because you didn't use an oven mitt. Do I need to continue?" I groan. Ok maybe it's true but it's not like I'm trying to get myself hurt.

"Emilia!" My mom shouts from downstairs. She sounds concerned. I hope everything is ok.

I sit up and respond, "Yeah?!" My mom runs up the stairs.

She's out of breath but she enters my room with a worried expression, "Emilia, when was the last time you've talked to Alice?" Huh?

I tilt my head, "At school right before March break started, why?" Oh she must've got that flu going around. I heard Anwen and Catarina got it last week. Maybe I can drop off some candy to help her feel better.

"Is Alice okay?" Cate asks.

My moms brows furrow, "Her parents just called, Alice is missing." Missing...? My eyes widen, Cate looks at me with concern. Missing...?
"If anything weird happened before March break started that you can remember, please tell me." I nod. My bedroom walls, seemingly shrinking until it becomes suffocating. This can't be happening . Alice was always so careful... What happened? Not to mention the Anti-Peace group on John and Block Street. Someone should've seen her get taken or leaving. Alice, I hope you're ok... my mom leaves my room to go downstairs.

Cate places his hand on my shoulder, "Are you ok?"

Am I? "I don't know."

<div align="center">~~~~~</div>

March break comes to an end and Alice is nowhere to be found. I head back to school where I see Anwen sitting on one of the rocks underneath the trees.

"Hi, Anwen." I force a smile.

She looks up at me with tired eyes, "Hi..."

"You look tired" I say. I'm tired too.

She nods, "Alice is my childhood friend, she's been there for everything. She was coming to my house...she never made it." Tears well up in Anwen's eyes.

I sit down beside her, "I know... I'm sorry." It's not my fault. I had nothing to do with it. But I'm the Saviour. I should've known, even if I couldn't't've. The bell rings and we go to get in line. Ms. Carvenon leads us up the six flights of stairs to class. One by one we sit at our desks. Two more empty desks. Catarina left during the beginning of the month, and Alice... it feels empty without them. Anwen's eyes are glassy, her posture is slouched. I hope Alice is ok.

As always, Ms. Carvenon walks to the front of the class, this time with a solemn expression, "As many of you may know, Alice Coelho has gone missing over the March break." Looking around, no one looks surprised. I take my hearing aids out of my fanny pack and put them in the ding of them turning on no longer sounding so cheerful.

"A therapist is coming to the school today so if you wish to speak with her, you may after lunch." Anwen starts trembling, I discreetly unzip my fannypack again. I take out a small candy and place it in her desk. It's not much, but I hope it'll make her feel a little better.

"Seeing the recent events, we'll be having a different class today." I wonder what that means.

"In the past ten years, young girls have been getting abducted at much higher rates across the globe." I tense up.

"Does anyone know the reason for this?"

Kala raises her hand, "Does it have to do with the Saviour." I tense up further. Is it my fault that these girls are getting taken...?

Ms. Carvenon nods, "That is correct. First world countries, second world countries, third world countries, rogue nations and corporations all want to discover or rather, create the next Saviour.

That is why girls are getting abducted." Does that mean... if I revealed myself as the Saviour... would Alice still be here?

"Of course, as you may have guessed, a Saviour cannot be created, however that doesn't stop others from trying." Did Lila die because of me...?

"Then there's the uprise in general child abductions. Does anyone know why boys and girls under the age eighteen are being abducted at such high rates?"

"Because they trusted the man with the white van giving out candy?" Louis laughs. Silvia laughs quietly too. She wonders why she has no friends yet she laughs at stuff like this.

"Very funny, I'm sure you'll find it even funnier in the principal's office. Now go." Ms. Carvenon says sternly. Louis tenses up.

"I said, now go." Louis gets out of his desk and leaves the class.

"The reason those under eighteen are trafficked at more alarming rates is due to Specialty Magic."

Anwen tenses up, she must be worried about Anastasia, "Children with appealing Specialty Magic are very valuable to our society. This is why they get trafficked." But why...?

"When the bodies of these children were found, the one thing they all had in common was that they all had their core's stolen." I feel sick.

"That being said, please be sure your parent or guardian picks you up from school. It is important that you don't walk home alone."

Eighteen days pass by, Alice is still missing. The white walls, though covered with the Lupo children's artwork, don't feel as warm as they had before.

"Emilia? Want some popcorn?" Catarina pushes the popcorn bowl towards me.

I smile and nod, "Thanks, can you believe we got detention 'cause Louis threw a half eaten corn dog at Max?" I put some popcorn in my mouth.

Diana giggles, "At least he didn't throw it at Anwen." Oh true, Anwen would've annihilated his past, present and future

Anwen grins her signature creepy grin, "If he threw it at me, I would curse his entire bloodline." I take another kernel. We laugh together for the first time in Eighteen days.

Catarina sighs, "Ok guys, serious talk." We all listen attentively to what she has to say.
"Did you see Aaron try to use light magic? He ended up flashbanging three teachers!" I choke on my saliva. Us four burst out laughing. I'm glad we're able to have a sleepover like this again.

Diana gasps for air, "Emilia, you should've shown him how it's done. You're our resident light magic user."

I force a smile, "I'm definitely not that goo-."

"Better than Aaron." Anwen quips. I start shaking with laughter. I make dim little fireworks in the air, showing off my magic.

"Thanks for not flashbanging us." Diana jokes.

I smile, for real this time, "It's really not that hard." I pull the brown blanket beside me over my legs.

Catarina grins, "Not that hard, huh? You just need Aether Magic and you'd have all the skills needed to be the next Alyssa Sawyer."

"I'm not that good. Plus, I'm nothing like what people say Alyssa was like. She's pretty much a saint!" I say.

Anwen laughs, "Yeah and you can't even get along with Damon."

"I uh, actually fought him during the simulation in February." I mutter.

"You what?!" My friends yell. Well that's a big reaction.

"Yeah... I'm surprised he hasn't tried to push me down the stairs yet." I say lightheartedly. That's a lie, I'm surprised I'm still alive.

Diana rushes closer to me, "Ok, spill the beans. What happened?"

"We finished beating each other's Nightmares and then he was being rude and shoved me. I shoved him back and then we started hitting each other." I say, getting quieter with each word.

"No wonder he's been glaring at you!" Anwen cackles.

Catarina sighs, "This is nice, if only Alice were here." Our shoulders slump.

Anwen responds, "Yeah... If only..." her eyes tearing up. Thanks for bringing down the mood, Catarina.

"Maybe we can each share our favourite memory or thing about Alice?" Diana suggests.

Anwen wipes away her tears, "I'll go first. Alice has always been there for me, through every birthday, every milestone, and every school year. I'll forever be grateful she was- is my friend."

Diana goes next, "Alice has always had my back and helped me when I needed help. My favourite memory of her is when she threw her slushy at Dominic last year because he stole my shoes and threw them over the fence." We all chuckle.

I sniffle, "Alice understood me better than anyone, I'll always be grateful that she made me feel safe and accepted."

"When I first moved to St Michael's, she showed me around and yelled at Aaron who tried to trip me. She always defended me when I couldn't defend myself."

Cold hands touch my shoulders, "You handle my power far better than my previous contractor. I'm impressed." Why can't A. leave me alone? Also 'contractor'? What does she mean by that?

"That Serbian Saviour, I think she was number seven or eight, well, you know how she turned out." Is she talking about Vlasta?

"I'm going to the washroom" I announce. Getting up from the air mattress, I walk past the island to the washroom, I close the door.

Turning to A. I ask, "What do you mean by that?"

She laughs, "I made a deal with her like I did with you, silly. She wanted to do her duty as the Saviour so badly, she practically signed everything away!"

She stops laughing, "You Saviours are so naive, you think you're doing the right thing but you have no idea. You're led around like dogs, it's pathetic."

I grit my teeth, "Is that how you see us? As dogs?"

She stops in her tracks, "What else would you be?" I scoff and leave the bathroom, putting on a smile. Walking back, I sit down in my original spot.

Anwen sighs, "We should probably try to move on."

"Move on?" Diana asks.

Anwen nods, "There's no way Alice is still alive, we should make peace with that and move on."

"They haven't found her body yet though…" Catarina says.

"They haven't found Lila's body either but we all know she's dead." Anwen snaps.

"Right… sorry." Catarina responds. Alice, wherever you are, I hope you're not in pain.

Chapter 26

The bell rings, signalling the end of the school day. For some reason I'm really tired. I walk out the north entrance, having been dismissed 5 minutes ago. Going past the blue doors I see my mom waiting by the car. I wave and run up to her, "Mom! Hi!"

She smiles and hugs me, "How was school today?" She seems to be in a good mood.

"It was good, Louis threw a half eaten sandwich across the room and Ms. Carvenon gave him detention." I respond, getting in the backseat of the car.

My mom gets in the driver's seat, "That sounds like an eventful day."
She starts the car and begins to drive, "Your father will be home late tonight but your brother is here so you should spend some time with him."

I grin, "Oppa is here?!" My mom laughs and nods. I can't believe my brother is back so soon! I've missed him a lot. I wonder if he has any more stories to tell. After about fifteen minutes, we arrive home. I open the doors of the black SUV and unlock the fence to enter the backyard. My mom walks in front of me and opens the door. My dog, Vanilla, is scratching at the door. Mom opens the door and out rushes Vanilla. She's jumping on me and licking my hands. She's so cute. I enter my house, taking my shoes off at the entrance. The sound of footsteps coming down the stairs can be heard. That must be Oppa!

"Oppa!" I shout.

My brother enters the back room, "Hey, kiddo. How've you been?"

I smile, "Good! I've been doing really well in my classes!"

He smiles back, "That's great! It wouldn't be good to have a Saviour that's sucky at her job. Don't you agree?" I nod eagerly and he ruffles my hair which has grown past my ears.
"I know you couldn't come to the tournament so... wanna see the videos I saved of it?" He's gonna show me the tourney footage? He's never shown me the tourney footage. I have to take this opportunity!

I smile brightly, "Obviously!"

He grabs the remote and goes to sit on the couch, "Come sit down." I sit down beside him and he connects his phone to the TV. The screen shows an arena with trees and poles. I watch in awe as my brother uses his lime green threads latch onto the poles and he uses it to slide himself across the arena. He's so cool! I wanna be just like him! His opponent, a tall guy with carbon black hair and bronze eyes, manages to dodge my brother.

"That's Eric. Dad told me you're classmates with his little brother."

Huh? Little brother? He can't mean, "You mean Damon?" Please let it not be Damon.

He nods, "Yep, Eric tells me a lot about him. He says Damon is quite the handful. How're you holding up with him in your class?" Crap. He is the last person I wanted to talk about with Oppa.

"It's uh, no big deal." I laugh awkwardly.

He chuckles, "I call bullshit, tell me what you really think."

"I want to pummel him." I say. Is that a bit much? I feel like that's a bit much. But he's so mean, I can't help it. It's not like I'll actually pummel him either...probably.

He laughs, "That bad?" I nod. My brother turns off the TV.

"Hey! Why'd you turn it off?" I whine. I wanted to see more!

"I can't have my little sister see me lose now can I?" He says.

I yawn. "Why don't you go take a nap, maybe we can go walk Vanilla at Low Park later?" I nod and head off to my room to take a nap. Climbing up the stairs, I make two lefts to get to my room. I flop onto my bed. I love my bed, it's so comfy.

"Hi, Emilia. Long time no see." Alice...? Is that you? I lift my head up to see Alice in my room. She smiles at me. Why is she here?

"Alice...?" I say, just above a whisper.

"I just wanted to say, I'm sorry." She says. Sorry for what?

Huh? "'Sorry'? Why are you sorry?"

She continues, "I hope we can still be friends." We'll always be friends.

"Alice, what do you mean? What's happening?" I ask pleadingly.

She ignores my pleas, "Don't go to Low Park later today." I open my eyes and sit up from my bed, gasping. What was that? Was that really Alice? It can't be...

"Oi, Kiddo." My brother pokes his head into my room.

I guess he sees how shaken up I am 'cause he says, "Oh, hey, are you ok?"

"Yeah, I'm fine... just had a bad dream." I mumble. Am I fine? I don't think I'm ok.

His eyes soften, "Maybe we can go around the block instead?" I smile and nod. I get out of bed and follow my brother down the stairs where Vanilla is waiting for us, her tail is wagging and she starts pawing at the door. He puts her harness on and we start walking. We pass various houses, some of them town houses, some of them apartments. Something feels off. Maybe I can ask to go to Low Park after.

"What was your dream about?"

How do I tell him? "I don't remember, it was just really scary." Hopefully he doesn't catch my lie. He nods and we continue walking. We finish the rest of the walk in silence, the sun is setting and we go back home. Once we walk into the house, I see my mom frantically texting on her phone. She looks really stressed. I tense up.

"Is everything ok?" My brother asks.

My mom turns to look at us, "Emilia... can you come here?" I nod hesitantly and walk over.

She hugs me tightly, "I'm so sorry, Emilia. I'm so sorry." Why is everyone sorry today? What's going on?

"Mom...?" What is she talking about?

She gets to my level and looks at me with sad eyes, "Emilia...They found Alice..." That dream wasn't a dream, was it... "She and Lila were found dead in one of the trails at Low Park. I'm so so sorry." My vision becomes blurry and my cheeks are wet. I sniffle. She hugs me tight. They're dead? Is that why she told me not to go to Low Park? Because her body was there...? My brother comes over and places his hand on my shoulder as I sob.

~~~~~

It's been three days since Alice and Lila's bodies were found. Two days ago their families announced they'd be having a joint funeral for the two of them. Alice and Lila were good friends after all. I put on my black dress and head downstairs where my family is waiting for me. This shouldn't be happening.

"You ready to go?" My mom asks. I nod and we get in the car. The drive is long, or maybe it's short. I can't tell. My surroundings pass by in a blur. Everything is moving too fast. Soon enough we arrive at the funeral home. I see the Lupo's and the Petrova's all there along with all my classmates and people in my grade. The funeral starts in half an hour so my mom tells me I can talk with my friends.
~~~~~

I walk up to Anwen, "Hi... how're you holding up?"

She looks down at me, "It's a closed casket funeral."

What? "Huh?" What does that have to do with how she is?

She continues, "On the news... Lila and Alice weren't found in one piece."

Her voice starts shaking, "They were dismembered so badly that they weren't able to put them back together. Lila's body was rotting..." My eyes widen. They were dismembered?

"But at least there are bodies to bury, right?" I nod hesitantly. We shouldn't be thankful for what should be the bare minimum. I know many Reverie's aren't given proper burials but Lila and Alice weren't Reverie's.

"Some people don't even get that..." I hug her and she sniffles, gripping the length of her black dress. It's going to be ok, it's going to be ok, it's going to be ok. No matter how many times I tell myself that, I can't bring myself to believe it.

I can't tell her what Alice said but I can at least say this, "Alice loved her friendships more than anything. She'd be so happy that you care about her this much." Diana and Catarina arrive, they walk over to us. They look like they're in bad shape.

Catarina forces a smile, "I didn't think the next time we'd see each other outside of school would be at a funeral..." Last time we said we'd move on, that way her death wouldn't hurt as much. So why does it feel like we lost her all over again?

Diana wipes her eyes, "This will be the last time all five of us are together in one place." I grit my teeth as my eyes start to water and my vision gets blurry. This can't be the last place we're all together, it can't be.

It's not fair! She smiles a broken smile, "Let's make the most of it." I know we should send Alice off with a smile. I know we should. But I can't bring myself to smile knowing she was until recently... Anwen said only Lila's body was rotting... the fact that she didn't say that Alice's body was, means she was likely killed within twenty-four hours of when they were found. Low Park is a busy park, someone would've noticed a body really quickly. She was still alive four days ago... I can't tell my friends that though. They're already hurting enough. I'm sure Anwen knows though. She's always been one to connect the dots. I look over to my left to see Mari crying into her mom's embrace. She was good friends with Lila so I can imagine this hurts a lot for her too. We start heading inside the funeral home. Despite all the paintings and flowers everything looks dull. I go to sit with my parents and brother. Soon enough Alice's mom starts to speak. She tells us how Alice may be gone but she'll never be forgotten and how she had hoped to be a professional gymnast if not a talented Reverie. Does she know that Alice was alive four days ago? Do they know that she was still alive when they gave up searching for her? Lila's dad starts talking next. He reminisces on how Lila was always so friendly, even when people weren't friendly back. How she made lots of friends and how grateful he is that his daughter was so loved by her peers. I space out, not wanting to hear more about how Alice and Lila were. I don't want to be here. I want to go home. I want to see Alice again.

My brother shakes my shoulder, "C'mon, we're going to bury the caskets now." I nod and get up. Walking across the ugly green carpet and past the pews. The adults carry the caskets outside. I can't bring myself to look at it. Alice and Lila's graves are beside each other. In front of the graves are two tables with white lilies. We're all instructed to take two. Tears run down my face as they're both lowered into the ground. Why did it have to be this way? Why were they kept alive for so long?

I take my two white lilies and I go to Lila's grave, "I'm sorry I didn't notice anything was wrong." I drop the white lily onto her casket and walk over to Alice.

"Thank you for being my friend. I will always remember you." I sniffle and drop my second white lily on top of her casket. Your dreams were taken from you and I am so sorry.

I look around, my brother is talking with Eric Petrova. Anwen is talking with Damon who looks surprisingly sympathetic. I look at the white lilies scattered across the two caskets. I need to be better. I need to be smarter. That way this won't ever happen again.

"How're you feeling?" My dad asks from behind me.

I force a smile for him, like I always do, "Alice and Lila aren't suffering anymore. That's a good thing. They must've been so scared." I lie through my teeth but that seems to be a good enough answer for my dad. Alice and Lila shouldn't be in the ground, they should be here. Lila should've been telling Marin about her crush on Aaron and Alice should've been coming with our group to get slushies. It's not fair.

Chapter 27

I open the front door of my home to see Cate carrying something big, "Hi hi! What's that you got there?"

Cate enters my house, his mom waving bye from the car, "I told you I had a surprise." I tilt my head.

"I started teaching myself to play the saxophone." Woah, that's so cool! He grins.

"It's actually quite comprehensive, although the reed isn't very pleasant." That's even cooler! I love the saxophone! It's such a great instrument.

I grin back, "You're the only person I know who can teach yourself a whole new instrument."

He takes off his shoes, "By the way, how are you holding up?"

Oh... he's talking about Alice, "I'm ok, I mean, I should be ok. It's been almost a month since the funeral after all."

I force a smile, "It's just... everyone is moving on... things are going back to normal. It's like Lila and Alice were never here to begin with."

"Studies show that it takes at least six months for grief to go away. It's perfectly normal that you're still grieving." He walks over to the couch and places his saxophone case down,

"Everyone has to move on eventually. Even if others forget them, you'll remember and they'll always have a place in your heart." Even if that's true, they deserved more. They deserved a life.

"Thanks." I say and follow him.

He sits down by the piano against the wall, "I also taught myself to play the piano."

My eyes widen and I smile, for real this time, "Wait, really?!"

He nods, "Maybe I can be your accompaniment for your recital."

"That would be so fun! I'll ask my teacher about it!" I exclaim.

He opens the lid of the piano, "We can practice now if you want? What song are you playing?"

I rush to the other corner of the room, almost tripping on one of Vanilla's toys, "I'm playing Ode to Joy." I grab my violin case and place it on the ground. Opening it, I take it out of the case and hook the shoulder rest on. I grab the bow and tighten it, then apply another layer of rosin on it. This is so exciting, I never thought Cate would be my accompaniment.

"Ode to Joy... I can do that." He says. Picking up my violin I get in my ready position. He starts the introduction. It's a bit clumsy but at the same time, surprisingly well done considering he's never played the song before. Once the introduction is done I join in. My fingers moving to hit the notes and my bow moving flawlessly. Cate starts speeding up. What is he doing? I speed up to try and keep up with him. He sticks his tongue out at me. Oh, he's doing this on purpose. I start speeding up my playing too. He speeds up to match me. We finish the song out of breath from trying to out play each other.

I laugh, "Thanks, I feel a lot better now."

He laughs with me, "So, am I good enough to be your accompaniment?"

I nod, "Obviously, but if you do that at the recital, I'm coming for your kneecaps."

"Aye aye, captain." He salutes me. I put my violin away and move to sit on the couch. Flickers of light dance in front of me. I tap each flicker, causing them to burst like fireworks.
"I always wanted to learn light magic."

I continue 'popping' the light, "Your magic is cool too."

He pulls out a hair, "Cool is subjective and I don't want to go bald." He transforms the strand of hair into a moon jellyfish.

It floats towards me and I tap it back to Cate's direction, "You could start bringing scissors with you so you can cut your hair instead of ripping it out."

"Maybe sheers?" He says while poking. The jellyfish towards me. There's a knock on the door. It must be Anwen!

I go to open the door, "Hi, Anwen!"

She smiles, "Hello." She comes in and I put my shoes on. Cate does the same.

My mom comes down the steps, "Oh, hello Anwen, Cato. Are you guys ready to go?" We nod and leave the house with my mom.
"So what store did you kids want to see again?"

"There's a new magic items shop nearby." Cate answers.

Anwen grumbles, "My sister won't let me have her old magic stones."

"So I was hoping to get some from there." We walk up the block to the Junction and turn right. Passing a few shops before we get to the one we want.

"I need to get something from the store beside this one, once you're done just wait for me outside." My mom tells us.

"Ok!" I say. We enter the store, the ding of a bell can be heard. The store is well lit and there are lots of tables and racks. Anwen heads straight for the gem section while Cate stays with me. It's a quaint shop, we start walking around. The light blue walls give the shop a friendly atmosphere.

"What are you looking for?" Cate asks.

I look up, "Hm, maybe a necklace or something? I know Anwen is secretly looking for a dagger." Anwen tenses up and slowly walks away from the dagger section. I think she's hoping we wouldn't notice. There are tons of gems, necklaces, rings, bracelets and more. It's hard to choose what I want.

"What do you want?"

"While there are many options to choose from, I believe the most strategic choice would be a mana amplifying ring." Cate says.

"A necklace is significantly easier for an opponent to take off and an ear cuff would get in the way." Of course he'd be worried about practicality. I just want something pretty that I can also use. Passing the gemstones area, I go deeper into the store. I get to the necklace section while Cate stays in the ring area. My eye catches onto one, it's a silver pendant with prongs holding a pink gemstone in place. This one is really pretty. I pick it up. It feels good in my palm and it has a good vibe to it. Wouldn't wanna get a haunted artifact or anything. The design is nice and it's pretty light. I take my findings up to the register.

The young woman behind the cashier smiles at me, "What are you interested in buying?" I show her the necklace and she nods in understanding. She seems nice.
"What's your name?"

Something tells me I shouldn't tell her my actual name, "My friend calls me Millie." She nods again and rings up the necklace.

The lady sighs, "You seem like a sweet girl, Millie. I can only wonder why such a pure soul like you has died countless times." I tense up. What did she just say? I can see Anwen tensing up too from the corner of my eye.
"I can only hope your spirit is one day able to find peace."
I think she noticed how stiff I am 'cause she continues, "You can have that necklace for free. It's the least I can do for such an unfortunate child."

I look down at the necklace in my palm then back at her, "Thank you." I walk to the front of the store and wait for Cate and Anwen to finish. That was so weird. Am I going to die? I mean, we all die at some point so that was really weird.

Chapter 28

"Mimi! What slushy are you gonna get after school today?" Mari says. Since Catarina left the class, Mari moved desks to sit in Catarina's old one. Although she swapped the position of the desk. None of us felt comfortable with anyone occupying Alice's old spot.

"If we ever get let out of this hold and secure then I'll start thinking about it." I groan. What's going on outside that we can't leave the school? I mean we've only been in the hold and secure for 10 minutes but Ms. Carvenon is really quiet so I'm getting kinda suspicious.

Anwen slumps on her desk, "It's so hot in here. I wanna leave."

I laugh, "We can't get the slushies now anyways even if we weren't stuck here since school is still going on."

My vampire looking friend lets out a loud groan, "I know."

Mari chimes in, "Well I want to get a cola flavoured slushy." That sounds good, I wonder what flavour I should get? "Do you know what flavour Cato likes?"

I nod, "He's more of an icecapp person. He's gonna meet us at the gas station."

"Cato drinks coffee?" Anwen asks. Right, I forgot that she only drinks tea.

"Yep, it's an Ecuadorian thing. We tend to drink coffee pretty young." I explain. Cate may be adopted but he's being raised with the same culture as me. It's kinda cool how his parents are also Korean and Ecuadorian. Although his Dad is Ecuadorian and his mom is Korean which is the opposite of me. "Obviously he's not drinking espresso shots but he occasionally drinks a bit of coffee."

Mari raises an eyebrow, "How much is a bit?"

"Honestly it's more milk and sugar than actual coffee. Icecapps are actually the strongest he drinks." I respond.

"Oh my god, enough about coffee. Why are all your friends annoying ass losers?" Silvia says from behind me. I roll my eyes.
"Honestly, you should be thanking whoever took Lila and Alice away. Two less insufferable people in this world." Mine and Mari's eyes widen. What did she just say?

Anwen grits her teeth, "You know, you never do know when to keep your mouth shut."

"And what're you gonna do about it? Hurt me? With what magic?" Silvia taunts. Anwen reaches into my desks and grabs my scissors, cutting a chunk of her hair from the back of her head. Silvia's eyes widen. Oh my god. Is this really happening?

Anwen smiles and places the scissors and clump of hair on Silvia's desk, "Ms. Carvenon!" Silvia's face contorts into an ugly expression.

"Silvia just cut my hair!" Silvia swats the hair and scissors away but they fall all around her desk.

Ms. Carvenon looks up from her work and scowls, "Miss Beek, what do you think you're doing?"

Silvia shrieks, "This bitch did it to herself! I didn't do anything!"

Our teacher's face turns stern, well, more stern than normal, "Come with me, you're going to the principal's office." She stands up and walks to the door. Silvia doesn't move.

"Either you go or I bring the principal here. The choice is yours." Silvia glares at Anwen and gets up from her desk, walking out of the class. Ms. Carvenon leaves with her.

"If I come back to a messy classroom, you'll all be cleaning it up." Once they leave, me and Mari go over to Anwen. This day is turning out to be crazy.

"I can't believe you just did that." I whisper.

"I know right!?" Mari whisper-yells.

Anwen sighs, "She deserved it after everything she's done and said."
She twirls one of her longer strands of hair, "Now, as for what slushy I want, I want a root beer one." I wonder how Mr. and Mrs. Lupo are gonna react to Anwen's new haircut.

"Guys, it's almost the end of the school year, that means the Lucid Ceremony is coming up!" Mari exclaims. Right, I can't believe time has passed by so quickly. It's hard to believe that a year ago we hadn't even seen a Nightmare before.

I pop a candy from my desk in my mouth, "I wonder which and how many of us will get a crystal." The candy melts in my mouth.
"I mean, the acceptance rate is usually around two percent."

"Us three will definitely make it." Anwen says. She's still twirling her hair. "And probably Damon."

Mari tilts her head, "Didn't Mimi and Damon beat each other up?"

"Hey! You're not supposed to say that out loud!" I whisper yell. Seriously, I told her not to mention it.
"Mari, if Damon goes down for that reason, I probably will too. So shh."

Mari nods, "Right, right. Shh." She places her finger to her mouth. Ms. Carvenon enters the room again and goes to sit back at her desk. Loud noises can be heard from Block Street.

I get up from my desk to look out the window, "Guys, get over here." I beckon Anwen and Mari over. In the distance, swat cars can be seen. There's a ton of police.

People are chanting, "The Saviour is gone! We need to kill them before they kill us!" and "They kidnapped the Saviour! We must get her back!" Police are dispersing the crowd and arresting people who are attacking them. Many are shielding a man in the middle. I wonder who that man is and why he's being shielded. The police and swat team push through and yank the man out, pinning him to the ground and arresting him. They then drag him off into one of the vehicles.

"What's going on?" Mari asks.

"I think that's the leader of the anti-peace group." Anwen says.

We both look at her before she continues, "Some people think he's the one who kidnapped Alice and Lila." That's the guy who did it? That can't be right. He's skinnier than Cate, how would he have been able to keep two kids under control like that? I can't imagine people are easy to dismember. So how could this guy pull all of that off?

"I want to believe this guy did it. Alice and Lila could finally get justice that way. But my gut is telling me they're arresting the wrong guy and I think they know it too."

Mari looks back at the scene, "Why would they knowingly take an innocent man?" The anti-peace group starts dispersing. I agree, why would they do that to someone they believe is innocent?

Anwen responds, "The police have been under a lot of fire because they haven't been able to find who took Alice and Lila." That makes a lot of sense.

I nod in understanding, "So they want to just catch someone so people will stop complaining?"

"That's probably the case, yeah." Anwen nods. We head back to our desks. The heat in the class is getting kinda uncomfortable. Outside there's a cool breeze so the heat isn't as bad. Soon enough the bell rings and an announcement comes on the speakers.

Mr. Norris starts speaking, "The hold and place has now been lifted, you are all now free to go." I get up and follow Mari to the cubbies. Grabbing my backpack, I head out of the class with my friends and we begin walking down the hallway. Turning the corner we start going down the first of the six flights of stairs.

"Hopefully Cate isn't there yet, 'cause we'll be at least ten minutes." I think out loud.

Anwen laughs, "Cato can handle himself for ten minutes."

Mari nods. "It's not our fault his school ends an hour early." We continue down the steps then turn the corner and push past the doors into the lobby.

"Time to venture forth." I announce. Anwen rolls her eyes playfully and Mari chuckles. Going past the office, we exit the school. We get to the fence and turn left so we're walking beside it. We pass by a few houses and the candy place which is actually a comic place but they sell candy for really cheap.

Anwen asks, "You guys didn't want any candy?"
I shake my head and Mari shrugs. We make it to the crosswalk with a bunch of other schoolmates. Everyone's chattering. I take my hearing aids off as we cross. People are too loud and the car engines are even louder. I place the hearing aids in my container and put it in my

fannypack. We walk past the pizza place and down the slight hill towards the gas station.

Mari lets out a noise of excitement, "We're so close to the slushies I can almost taste it!" Me and Anwen laugh as we turn to get to the entrance of the gas station. Cate is standing outside the entrance with his backpack.

I wave and rush over to him, "You didn't have to wait outside, you know? It's like twenty-seven degrees out."

He grins, "Actually with the wind chill it feels like twenty-five degrees so some could argue that it's not that bad out."

"Twenty-seven is still twenty-seven. Now let's go and grab our slushies before I melt into the pavement." Anwen walks inside. We all follow her. Me, Anwen and Mari walk to the slushy area while Cate goes to the coffee shop part of the gas station to get an icecapp. I grab a medium cup and fill it with the cream soda flavour.

Mari grabs the cola flavour, "I will devour you and love every moment."

Anwen stops filling her cup, "To really strike fear, you should tell it about how you'll end its bloodline." She continues to get her root beer slush. I walk to the cash register to pay. I give the cashier a twoonie and I get some change back. Leaving the building, I join Cate who's waiting outside again.

"What flavour icecapp did you get?" I ask. He probably got the sweetest flavour they have.

He answers, "It's actually an Iced Capp not icecapp, and I got the s'mores flavour." Bingo, I was right.

I hold out my slush, "I don't think you've had cream soda before, I'll let you try mine if I can try your ninety-five percent sugar-milk mixture." He agrees and we swap drinks. Both taking a sip of each others.

"This is good." He says.

I grimace as I taste the icecapp, "This is diabolical." We give each other our drinks back.

"Your tastebuds just haven't matured yet." He says a little too confidently.

I take a sip of my glorious cream soda slush, "Says the one who's drinking mostly sugar and milk. Coffee is gross no matter what form it's in."

Anwen and Mari come out and Cate's eyes widen, "Anwen, what happened to your hair?" I kinda forgot she cut it to be honest.

She furrows her brows and squints, "What do you- Oh, right. Justice happened."

"Justice? Actually I don't think I need to know." He responds.

"Good choice." Anwen says.

Chapter 29

The day has finally arrived, June twenty-third. The Lucid Ceremony is here!

I'm practically vibrating out of my seat when my brother says, "Chill out, shrimpy. We'll get there soon enough."

I stop moving, "But Oppa! Today's the day!"

"You sure are excited." My dad says, looking at the road ahead as he drives.

"Of course I am!" I shout.

My brother winces, "Hey, hey, shh. You don't need to be so loud."

"Now Emilia, you know only one of us is allowed inside. Your brother said he'll go but just know me and your father will be eagerly awaiting your results." My mom looks back at me from the front seat.

"Whatever your results are, we'll still love you." She smiles and looks forward.

"I'm sure you'll make it, kiddo. You got some real nice Specialty Magic, and you're the Saviour. Not to mention dad told me your grades are pretty good." My brother ruffles my hair. Soon enough, we arrive at the school. Me and my brother get out of the car while my mom and dad go to park. We walk into the north yard where my classmates' parents and some friends are waiting. I see Catarina in the distance.

She waves at me, "Good luck, Emilia!"

I wave back, "Thank you!"

"That a friend of yours?" My brother asks. I nod and we head inside, passing by the grade eight classroom. We enter the gymnasium where I see Anwen and Mari. Diana is over in the corner by the corkboard with Kaine and Silvia. Why there's a corkboard in the gym, I don't know. Anastasia is talking with Eric who's watching Damon like a hawk. "You gonna be ok with your friends?" The room is filled with chatter.

I give him a thumbs up, "Yep!"

Oppa holds out his fist, "I'm going to go talk to Eric, call me if you need me." I bump his fist with my own and he walks over to the Petrova's and Anastasia. I wonder why Anastasia is close with Eric. I mean, I'm not that close with any of my parents' family friends. I wonder if I'll be able to become friends with other Academy students like that.

"Emilia!" Mari waves at me. I walk over and hug her.

Turning to Anwen, I ask, "Why is Anastasia with Eric Petrova?"

"Oh, he's her mentor, that's why." She responds.

"Mentor?" Me and Mari question.

Anwen nods, "Yeah, the Academy has a student mentor program where older students can mentor younger students. You have to sign up for that though." Ohh, that makes sense.

I look up at Anwen, "Do you know who my brother mentors? He never told me."

"Oh he mentors Adeline Petrova." She says nonchalantly. My brother mentors Adeline Petrova?! That's insane! Why wouldn't he tell me?! That's so cool! "Although it ended up like that 'cause of a favour." Me and Mari tilt our heads.
"Adeline got adopted by the Petrova's two or three years ago and Eric wanted her mentor to be someone trustworthy so he asked

your brother." That makes sense. The Elder comes into the gymnasium with his assistant.

He walks onto the stage, "May I get all the Academy candidates up on the stage?" It's finally happening! It's finally happening! All ten of us get on the stage and line up shoulder to shoulder. The anticipation in the air is thick enough to cut with a knife.

"You've all worked hard over the course of a year, and now you're here. Congratulations to all ten of you who made it to the end." His assistant brings out a tray. I assume the lucid crystals are on it.

"Now, it's time for you to find out whether you've earned your ticket to the Academy." I look down at my brother who's smiling at me, I smile back.

"There are ten of you standing here today and there are four crystals." Four?! Even two is a lot let alone four! I mean, sometimes no one gets a crystal. This is huge! I look around and see Mr. Reynard in the crowd. He looks like a proud parent watching his child's first steps, but also like he's really sad... weirdo.

My brother mouths, "I'm rooting for you, shrimpy."

Atticus continues to speak, "I will be going from right to left." His assistant stands beside him.

"If I touch your head you are free to get off the stage and head home if you so wish."

He places his hand on Louis's head then goes to stand in front of Anwen, "Despite your low mana count, you have shown time and time again that you have what it takes to enter the Academy. Congratulations, Anwen Lupo." He hands her a crystal. It turns a crimson red colour. He moves to stand in front of Max and places his hand on his head. Max leaves the stage. The Elder gets to Kaine and places his hand on her head. He gets to Mari,

"Marin Abdul, you are an impressive mix of both athleticism and magical talent. Congratulations on your entrance to the Academy." Mari smiles brightly as she receives her crystal that turns a pale blue colour.

He gets to me, "Emilia Jang, you may be lacking in strength and endurance, but your mana control far exceeds everyone here. Congratulations on your acceptance to the Academy." Oh my god I did it! I did it! I look at my brother who's giving me double thumbs up. The Elder gives me my crystal and it turns amethyst.

A taunting voice whispers in my ear, "Congratulations, Emilia. You'll be able to fulfill your end of the deal now." Why can't A. just leave me alone? I ignore her.

"Good luck. You'll need it."

The Elder moves in front of Kala and places his hand on her head, she moves offstage. Then it's Diana's turn. There's only one crystal left. Please let it not go to Silvia. He places his hand on her head. I raise my hand. My brother's eyes widen, people start murmuring.

The Elder pauses, "Yes, Emilia?"

All right, here goes nothing, "If you haven't fully decided on who to give the crystal to, then I nominate Damon Petrova." Silvia's eyes widen and she glares at me.

"And why is that?" He asks.

I respond, "Silvia is constantly saying horrible things and bullying others. She even pulled a knife on me once." Silvia's face fills with anger.
"I don't think someone like that should enter the Academy, especially since it might put people with lower resistance levels at risk." Damon's eyes widen in shock.

Silvia explodes in anger, "Who the actual hell do you think you are?! Why would they choose a Nightmare over me?! He's barely even human!"

Atticus's eyes narrow, "While I do not agree with the wording, I would like to know why I shouldn't just end the Ceremony here?" Silvia tenses up. Her outburst just caused her to lose her entrance, if it was ever on the table that is.

I take a deep breath, "Because as you know, I'm the Saviour." I fill the room with warmth and little bursts of light. Gasps fill the room.

Damon looks unsurprised while my other classmates stare at me with wide eyes. "Damon may be difficult and kind of a jerk, but he's not intentionally malicious. Plus, him being half Nightmare can work in our favour." Murmurs fill the room, I see my brother, Eric and Anastasia talking. Anastasia looks shocked while Eric seems to be enjoying this.

Atticus raises an eyebrow, "And what favour would a child like him bring?"

"I'm glad you asked, since he's half Nightmare, we can see how he fights and analyze him. Someone there must've trained him. Someone far stronger than a calibre ten. That person is a danger. Wouldn't having someone already strong like Damon be beneficial to us? Having him on our side would, in my opinion, help greatly." I respond.

He strokes his chin, "What if he betrays us? What do you propose we do then? And how will you justify the risk?"

I smile, "I'll assume responsibility if he betrays us. I'm the Saviour, it's my duty to serve my country. If Damon Petrova betrays us, I'll kill him. I'll consider him to be nothing more than a dangerous Nightmare in that scenario, I will hunt him down and kill him."

Atticus freezes and smiles, "I see you are dedicated to your role as Saviour and your duty to protect our country. Very well, I will hold you to that."

He places his hand on Silvia's head and walks in front of Damon, "Count yourself lucky. Congratulations on your entry to the Academy." He hands Damon a crystal that turns a rosy pink colour. Damon looks at me with utter shock on his face. I cannot believe I just did that.

"Congratulations to everyone who passed, you may leave now."

I get off the stage and my brother rushes up to me, "You really are full of surprises, but please, never do that again." I nod.

Mr. Reynard walks up to my brother, "Hello, my name is Reynard, I'm one of Emilia's teachers. I just came to say congratulations."

He turns to me, "Congratulations, Emilia, I hope to see whatever great things you achieve in the future." I smile.

My brother smacks my head, "What do you say, Emilia?"

I clutch the back of my head, "Ow." I turn to Mr. Reynard,

"Thank you very much." He laughs and waves goodbye. People start funneling out of the gymnasium and to the North yard where everyone is waiting. I rush to my parents and hug them.

"I did it!" I show them my lucid crystal. They hug me back.

"Congratulations, Emilia! I knew you could do it." My dad says.

My mom smiles, "See? Your hard work paid off in the end. Congratulations." I see Anwen waving at me.

"Can I go say 'hi' to Anwen?" I ask, my parents nod. I rush over to Anwen, "Hey, what's up?"

"I've been thinking." She says. She doesn't sound very excited.
"Being a Reverie, it's dangerous." I nod in agreement. "Promise me you'll survive?" My eyes widen.
"I already lost Alice, I don't want to lose another friend. Plus, you're the Saviour so you'll have to be in a lot of dangerous situations." She holds out her pinky.

I smile and link my pinky with hers, "I promise." She smiles. "Also, sorry for not telling you about the whole Saviour thing, the Elder told me not to tell people."

She nods, "I understand."

I continue, "Don't worry about me, I'll survive even if I have to claw through the intermedial and back."

"You better keep that promise, Emilia." She says. We both smile and walk back to our families. "I will survive, no matter what it takes."

A. whispers in my ear, "There is so much you don't know yet."

I look up towards the treeline, "Even so, it doesn't matter. I'll keep my end of the deal."

Acknowledgements

Thank you so much to my Beta readers;

Greene Kinoshita, Collete Addison, Gerenz "Galaxy" Andal, Jermaine Marshall, Niko and SlugCatScarf. You guys were such tremendous help and this book wouldn't be nearly as good without your input.

A very silly thank you to the silliest guy around; MistyKoa. Thank you so much for editing this, you are a lifesaver

Lastly, a huge thank you to my illustrator; Michell Diaz. Your art is very yummy in my tummy and I look forward to seeing more of it.